"The Lavene duet can always be counted on for an enjoyable whodunit." — *Midwest Book Review*
"This jolly series...serves up medieval murder and mayhem." — *Publishers Weekly*
"[A] terrific mystery series." — MyShelf.com

MURDEROUS MATRIMONY

This story has a great mystery with plenty of suspects to keep us guessing – Fabulous characters including a ghost – Takes place in a fantastic setting. I love reading stories that leave me smiling at the end with a few giggles throughout and anxious for the next book.
~ Lori Caswell

The characters are undeniably funny and well thought out. I don't read many books other than Christian but found this one to be enjoyable and a clean read. I give Murderous Matrimony, book 6 in A Renaissance Faire Mystery Series, 5 stars.
~ Michelle Prince Morgan

PERILOUS PRANKS

This novella whets your appetite for the next book in the Renaissance Faire Mystery series - Murderous Matrimony, coming in November 2013. This is a quick fun read. It will keep you turning the pages so you can find out whodunit. The story is well plotted and will keep you intrigued with quirky characters and red herrings galore. Well, Joyce and Jim have done it again - they never disappoint. So if you like your mystery with the fun of a Renaissance Faire, then you should be reading Perilous Pranks. — **Cheryl Green**

continued . . .

TREACHEROUS TOYS

The latest Renaissance Faire Mystery (see Harrowing Hats, Deadly Daggers and Ghastly Glass) is an engaging whodunit made fresh by changing the season as the heroine provides a tour of the Renaissance Faire Village during Christmas (instead of the summer). This exciting amateur sleuth (with Jesse's success rate on solving homicides while risking her life on cases the cops fumble; she should turn pro to pay her bills) is filled with quirky characters as team Lavene provide another engaging murder investigation. ~ Harriet Klausner

HARROWING HATS

"The reader will have a grand time. This is an entertaining read with a well-crafted plot. Readers of the series will not be disappointed. New readers will want to glom the backlist so they don't miss a single minute." — *Fresh Fiction*

"The Renaissance Faire Mysteries are always an enjoyable read . . . Joyce and Jim Lavene provide a complex exciting murder mystery that amateur sleuth fans will appreciate."
— *Midwest Book Review*

continued . . .

DEADLY DAGGERS

"The Lavene duet can always be counted on for an enjoyable whodunit . . . Filled with twists and red herrings, *Deadly Daggers* is a delightful mystery." — *Midwest Book Review*

"Will keep you entertained from the fi rst duel to the last surprise . . . If you like fun reads that will let you leave this world for a time, this series is for you." — *The Romance Readers Connection*

"Never a dull moment! Filled with interesting characters, a fast-paced story, and plenty of humor, this series never lets its readers down . . . You're bound to feel an overwhelming craving for a giant turkey leg and the urge to toast to the king's health with a big mug of ale as you enjoy this thematic cozy mystery!" — *Fresh Fiction*

GHASTLY GLASS

"A unique look at a renaissance faire. This is a colorful, exciting amateur sleuth mystery fi lled with quirky characters who endear themselves to the reader as Joyce and Jim Lavene write a delightful whodunit." — *Midwest Book Review*

continued . . .

WICKED WEAVES

"This jolly series debut . . . serves up medieval murder and mayhem." — *Publishers Weekly*

"[A] new, exciting . . . series . . . Part of the fun of this solid whodunit is the vivid description of the Renaissance Village; anyone who has not been to one will want to go . . . [C]leverly developed." — *Midwest Book Review*

Bewitching Boots

By

Joyce and Jim Lavene

Chapter One

A tall, older gentleman with a red cap called out the time and announcements as he walked through the Village carrying a wood staff with a lantern at the top. "Princess Isabelle approaches. All ye look upon her and tremble."

The voice of the crier was as excited by the news as I was. It wasn't bad enough that the royalty of Renaissance Faire Village and Marketplace couldn't walk the cobblestones without their retinues. They had to formally announce their presence too.

"She's beautiful!" Bill Warren stood beside me, gazing out the window of the Art and Craft Museum. "Who is she?"

I sighed at the awe in his tone. No wonder royalty had people announce who they were.

"That's Princess Isabelle." I watched her saunter toward us with ladies in fine, pastel summer gowns attending her, jugglers amusing her, and gorgeous young men doting on her. "She's the older princess at the castle. She's not actually the daughter of the king and queen like Princess Pea is. She's an actress, like a lot of other people around here."

Bill still held a piece of soft leather in his big hands. He was a shoemaker who'd recently opened a stall at the Village. He was in his fifties, a burly man with graying blond hair and peculiar pointed ears. I'd noticed his ears the first time we'd met when he doffed his feathered hat to me.

"I don't know who Princess Pea is," he continued, "but if she looks anything like Princess Isabelle, she's a wonder. What do you know about her?"

What could I say that wouldn't sound like sour grapes? Could I say that Isabelle used her beauty and power to cause trouble and torment people? That she ruined people's lives with her annoying habits of breaking hearts?

She was guilty on both counts. But mostly, I just didn't like her. She still flirted with Chase, my husband of almost a year, still trying to come between us. She was the bane of most women's lives in the Village. She didn't care who she hurt as long as she got her way.

I really didn't like her.

"No. Don't tell me about her." Bill pulled back from the window. "Let me find out about her, as I would a fine wine."

First of all—gagging. Second, she wouldn't give him a glance much less enough time to find out something personal about her.

I didn't want to tell him that. He was new here. He'd find out eventually what she was all about.

"She's so graceful. I'll bet she's a dancer."

"She dances," I agreed. "When it suits her."

We went back to setting up his exhibit in the museum. He'd brought dozens of pairs of boots, slippers, and moccasins with him. His craftsmanship and attention to detail was exquisite.

When I'd found him making boots on a trip to Tennessee, I immediately recruited him for the Village. I'd offered him, as the museum director, a guest spot at the museum as a way to introduce him. I hoped that he'd choose to stay with us. The Village lacked an old-fashioned cobbler.

I couldn't believe the laughs the word cobbler got me as I suggested the man to the king and queen. They had final say-so over new shops and artisans coming into the Village. It seemed the food form of cobbler had overtaken its original meaning as a person who cobbles shoes.

King Harold and Queen Olivia were still thrilled with the idea of having Bill there. They suggested calling him a shoemaker rather than a cobbler so as not to be confusing with pie.

I didn't bother again to explain the difference, even between pie and fruit cobbler. Let them think what they would.

"You were right about this place, Jessie." Bill set out his tools and materials on a large table. "I've already sold more boots in a week than I did in a month back home. Plus there are all the perks of living here. I rode an elephant three times yesterday. That will never get old."

"I'm sorry your shop wasn't ready when you got here. They say it should be finished by the time your exhibit is over." Most of the artisans and craft people in the Village lived in similar small houses with pointy roofs. Their homes were upstairs and shops on the ground floor.

"Not a problem. The stall is fine for now. I love your name for the shop by the way—Bewitching Boots." He glanced at me with one thick brow lifted. "It's more apt than you know."

I sorted through the soft boots to decide how best to display them. I'd already put hooks in the walls for some, but others I thought should lay out where people could see and touch them. "Yes? How's that?"

"My family has always been shoemakers. The Brother's Grimm wrote about us in their stories."

I stopped sorting. "What did they write?"

He kept working, setting up his table and equipment. His black britches and loose-fitting white linen shirt were well made and entirely appropriate. The boots he wore were an example of his wonderful work. They were black, slightly higher than his knee, with large, brass buckles on the sides.

"We were featured prominently in the story about the elves and the shoemaker. That was my great-great-great grandfather. There was some question about whether or not he took an elf as a wife. Either way, magic enhanced his career after that. We've been blessed with magic since then."

That didn't really surprise me. I lived and worked in a reproduction of a Renaissance village, and for the last year, we'd experienced some strange happenings. It had all started at the time of Wanda's death. She had become our resident ghost.

"We have a few witches here too. Not to mention our ghost."

He laughed. "I've seen her. She's one crazy female."

"You've seen Wanda?" Okay. That surprised me.

"Sure. Having a lineage of magic allows me to see things that other people might not be able to see."

"I wish I could give up that opportunity. Wanda has been a pain in the butt since she died. Not that she was any better when she was alive. Just that she gets around more now. I used to have to visit her. Now she finds me."

"She says she was murdered right here in the Village."

How much should I say about that terrible event? I didn't want to scare him off. "It's true. There was an unfortunate set of circumstances that caused her death. That kind of thing doesn't happen on a regular basis, though. No need to worry."

"I never worry about anything bad happening to me, Jessie. My magic keeps bad things away. That's how I'm able to put such good thoughts and happy feelings into my creations."

Magic was getting to be a commonplace thing here at the Village. Did he really have magic? I wasn't sure and didn't want to pursue it. I was still adjusting to the magic I knew was real.

"I guess that's why I've enjoyed the sandals you made for me." I lifted my long, red skirt a little so he could see them on my feet. "They're attractive, and very comfortable. It's not often you can find a size twelve sandal that fits so well."

Yes. I have large feet. But considering I'm also six feet tall—I need them to balance me.

"And don't you feel extra good while you're wearing them?" he asked.

I thought about it, not sure what he was looking for. "Yes. They're my favorites."

"I'll bet you get around faster in them too, without your feet hurting."

"Sure." I didn't know if that was true or not. I hadn't really noticed. But if he believed in what he was doing, who was I to disagree?

The door to the museum was flung open, letting in all the hot, humid air. It was summer in Myrtle Beach, South Carolina—home of Renaissance Faire Village. I'd finally managed to convince the maintenance people to put in some ceiling fans. At least in the mornings, the temperature stayed mild.

Air conditioning was out of the question, like cell phones, computers, and other modern devices. Except at the castle. It was blessedly cool there in the summer. Some of the resident housing had air conditioning too, but most only had fans.

"Here ye, hear ye." The man who was acting as Isabelle's presenter for the day began his announcements. "The beautiful and excellent Princess Isabelle cometh."

"Seriously?" I asked.

He shrugged. "That's what she said."

Isabelle came inside with her giggling ladies-in-waiting. She held her head high, her long black hair dressed with artificial pearls for the day. They matched her pearl-colored gown and reticule. She was tiny—petite—I think they call it.

One of the ladies carried a parasol to protect the princess from the sun. Another brought along two hand-painted fans to cool her fevered brow. Still another carried perfume and

other necessities to protect Isabelle's delicate nose. They all
stood to the side, heads bowed, as the princess walked past
them.

"How now, shoemaker?" Isabelle's tone was frosty
enough to cool the entire Village. "I have come to view your
wares. Show me your best, and quickly! I have no time to
dawdle."

A handsome redheaded gentleman with bright green
eyes and a tiny red beard found a chair for her. "You may
approach the princess now, shopkeeper."

Bill, for all his bulk, made a graceful bow to the
princess. He took her hand in his and delicately kissed her
fingertips. "Princess Isabelle. You honor me with your
presence."

"I know." She shook her hand after taking it back from
him and glanced away. The redheaded gentleman
immediately brought out a stoneware jar of hand sanitizer.
"I'm looking for a pair of slippers."

"Dancing slippers, I'll wager." Bill smiled at her as
though she really was a royal princess.

Some people get lost in the act.

"Yes. Exactly. How did you know?"

That was actually more than I'd expected Isabelle to say
to him. Maybe he was right about having magic.

Bill brought out a small, crudely made wood stool that
he placed close to her feet. "May I examine your present
slippers, Your Highness, as well as your beautiful feet?"

Isabelle actually smiled. I had to assume she was
mellowing in her approaching third decade. Maybe she was
actively trying to get people to like her. There was a rumor
that Princess Pea could replace her when she was old enough.
Isabelle still had time to make friends. Pea was only a baby.

"Off with you, shoemaker." The red-haired gentleman
nudged Bill hard. "No one touches the princess without her
express permission."

He had to be Isabelle's new boy-toy. I could have
warned him that she didn't appreciate men who tried to usurp

her authority. There was no prince in her life, and I was pretty sure she liked it that way.

"Be gone, Sir Dwayne." Isabelle banished him with a wave of her delicate white hand. "I am able to speak for myself."

"Of course, my lady!" Sir Dwayne put his hand to his heart as he bowed his head and slunk away to the back row of her followers.

Bill hadn't moved from his stool. He straightened his shoulders under the blousy white shirt and carefully lifted one of the princess's feet in his hands. "Like lovely, small birds." He admired her foot in the pale slipper.

Isabelle giggled. "Really, sir! Fie on thee for lying! My feet are the very worst part of me. It is an embarrassment for anyone to see them."

"Not at all, my lady." He slowly slipped off her shoe and placed it on the floor before he held her foot in both hands as he examined it. "Delicate, high arches. Sweet skin. Dainty toes. A foot, indeed, created for a princess."

Her retinue agreed with loving smiles.

I kept expecting Isabelle to lash out, kick Bill off the stool, or in some way make him look foolish. To my surprise, she was actually pleasant.

"How now, Sir Shoemaker! What are you saying?" She smiled sweetly and leaned closer to him, her hand resting lightly on his shoulder as her pale bodice dipped open near his eyes. "You have such a warm touch, sir. I swear it is making me quite giddy."

Bill whispered something in her ear as he slowly massaged her foot.

Whatever he said made Isabelle go quiet for a moment. Her face turned red, and her lips parted slightly as though in anticipation. She finally burst into peals of excited laughter. "Sir! You mistake me. I am not soliciting your attention with my peculiar digits. And we shall discuss that other, entirely ribald suggestion when you deliver my slippers to me at the castle."

He bowed his head and actually kissed her foot. It was a weird moment in shoemaker history, at least for me. "I shall deliver them as soon as they are finished. I promise you will dance the night away without a single moment of tired or aching feet. This I swear to you, Princess."

She giggled again as he took her measurements. When he was finished, he carefully put her shoe back on and helped her from the chair. "Until later, lady, when I come to fit your slippers." He kissed her hand again, slowly turning her palm up to plant the embrace.

All I can say is that I was glad he didn't do any of that when I bought my sandals from him. I wouldn't have asked him to come to the Village, and I didn't want to think how Chase would have taken it.

I took a sideways peek at Sir Dwayne. His face was almost as red as his hair. He wasn't taking the shoemaker's dalliance with Isabelle well. . The look he gave Bill promised hard times for him in the future.

Men came and went quickly in Isabelle's life. I wasn't too worried about my protégé. He might get his heart bruised in his encounter with her, but he'd no doubt survive. He couldn't have lived this long, especially with his impressive magic charm, without falling in and out of love.

Despite her rebuff, Isabelle looked for Dwayne to escort her from the museum when it was time to go. She rested her hand on his arm and gave him a flirtatious smile. Their nearly matching garments pegged them as a current couple

I curtsied as she started past me, glad that I'd been like a fly on the wall for her visit. Usually our meetings didn't end with smiles and kisses.

She paused, seeming to notice me for the first time since she'd entered the museum. Her lovely, fake smile was in place on her sun-blocked face. "Oh, there you are, Lady Jessie. Please give my regards to the Bailiff. Since you married, he doesn't seem the same. He was so happy once, but I suppose the wrong union can sour anyone."

"I shall give him your regards, Princess. He has spoken

of you in the past as part of a time best forgotten in his life. I'm certain he'll consider your greeting in the same fashion."

Isabelle didn't spare me another glance. She'd gotten in her dig for the day. So had I. She also didn't bother looking down or she would've noticed my sandaled foot immediately in her path. Sir Dwayne was on hand to keep her from a tumble.

Too bad.

Bill chuckled when she was gone, the last of her people following her slowly down the stairs to the cobblestones. "Quite a cat fight you almost had going there, Jessie. You two have history, I take it?"

"You could say that. She's always wanted my boyfriend—now my husband. She has so many men around her, I've never understood why. Not that Chase isn't irresistible, but it's like she can't stand that he's mine now."

"A woman like Isabelle can never be happy with only one man's regard. She needs constant reassurance that she's as radiant as a sunlit garden. It might seem redundant to tell her. She sees it in the mirror every day. But she needs reassurance as other women require fresh air and water. Not to worry. Now that I'm here, she'll give up the other men."

Oh brother!

I hung several pairs of boots with beautiful, elaborate stitchery on them. It was easy to believe Bill had magic in his fingers. I liked him too, which made me break my rule about warning him away from Isabelle. I really wanted him to stay in the Village. "You know, Isabelle may be her own worst enemy. She has a love'em and leave'em kind of reputation. I don't want to see you get hurt."

"You're a good friend, Jessie. Don't worry about me. I have elf magic."

It reminded me so much of the old Keebler cookie commercials from when I was a kid that I smiled. "I believe you. Just be careful."

He waggled his shaggy brows and wiggled his ears. "You'll see. When I set my sights on a lady, she can't resist me."

I'm not kidding. The man wiggled his pointed ears. I wasn't sure if it was funny or alarming. I'd never seen anyone who could wiggle their ears. Bill was indeed a man of rare talents.

We worked side-by-side finishing the setup on the museum exhibit. It was due to open the next day. Everything was ready for what I hoped would be a good crowd. Adventureland, the parent company for Renaissance Faire Village, was paying for a nice spread and publicity for the opening. It seemed they liked the idea of having a shoemaker there too.

The Main Gate opened for visitors at ten a.m. each day. I suggested that we break for coffee. I was meeting Chase and our friends, Daisy and Bart, at Sir Latte's Beanery. I invited Bill to join us, as he had many times while we'd been working on the exhibit.

"I can't come today," he said. "My brain is on fire with images of Isabelle's beautiful feet. I'm going to get started on her dancing slippers. I want to fit them on her as soon as possible. I want to feel her feet in my hands again."

That was a little more information than I needed on that subject, but I didn't say so. "That sounds great. I'll be back later, and we'll make sure everything is ready for opening day."

"Don't worry. It will be magical. I guarantee it."

I wondered why he hadn't mentioned having elf magic before. I'd known him a few weeks. We'd talked about all kinds of things. Magic seemed like something that would have come out sooner.

"Maybe not," Daisy said as we waited for Chase and Bart to join us for coffee. "Maybe he has to get to know you before he drops the M-bomb. Maybe he has to trust you. You know people used to do nasty things to those who professed a knowledge of magic."

Daisy was a sword, knife, and armor maker in the Village. Her shop, Swords and Such, was very popular with the hundred thousand or so visitors we received each year. Her adult son, Ethan, was working with her now too. Bart was her lover and now her partner in the shop. He was computer savvy and had opened an online version of her shop that outsold the bricks and mortar version ten times over.

"That was a long time ago, but maybe that's it." I shrugged. "I'm glad he didn't do the love at first sight with my feet thing that he did with Isabelle today. It was awkward watching it."

"I don't know." Daisy tossed her dyed blond curls, her lips drawn in a red bow, like a kewpie doll. She always wore a breastplate with a phoenix on it. "I like a good foot rub. Bart is fantastic at it—he's got those huge hands. Maybe I should stop in for a new pair of boots. Your cobbler sounds interesting."

"Cobbler?" Bart joined us. "Cherry or apple? I like both."

Chase, my lovely husband, had come into the crowded pub with Bart. He kissed me quickly before he sat beside me. "Not pie. Shoemaker. Jessie brought him back with us from Pigeon Forge when we went to Dollywood. He makes great boots." Chase held up one foot to show off his new pair of Bill's boots.

"He might be about to take Isabelle out of your fan club," I told him. "They really had something going on today at the museum."

Chase was a little skeptical. "Not to sound harsh, but I'm surprised she was interested in him."

"Why?" Bart asked.

"He's kind of plain, in his fifties or so." Chase thanked the server who brought his coffee. "Not exactly Isabelle's type."

Daisy grinned. "Jessie says he gives magical foot rubs. Sounds good to me. Maybe Isabelle is a gal who likes to play with feet."

Bart put one of his massive arms around her shoulders,

almost hitting a knave seated behind him. "I give magical foot rubs too. You don't need the pie man."

"He didn't give me a magical foot rub." Chase laughed. "Did he do that for you, Jessie? It must've been when I was looking around his shop. I might've noticed you playing footsies with him."

"Oh you newlyweds," Daisy protested. "What's a foot massage between consenting adults? I really can't wait to meet the cobbler now. Bart, don't you need a new pair of boots too?"

"Not if the shoemaker has to touch my feet. You know how ticklish they are."

We talked about the coming week. It was August, the time when dozens of college and high school students left the Village to go back to school. Many of them would return over Christmas and Spring Break, but we always needed replacements for the time between.

Renaissance Village was a big place to fill with interesting characters. Many of the college men were knights at the Field of Honor. We couldn't have jousts twice a day without knights.

"I guess they'll be in this morning." Daisy rubbed her hands together. "I love to antagonize the newbies. It shows their inner character. Let's face it—most visitors are more annoying than I could ever be."

We all pretty much agreed with that.

The selection of several dozen new actors was done by daily auditioning on the cobblestones. The regulars, such as Daisy and Bart, me and Chase, marked scorecards that were tallied to decide who would be invited back for the next day. Some would be chosen for their original costumes, but most would be chosen for their friendliness and willingness to act as though they belonged. At the end of the week, the players that remained would be selected.

"I'm glad all of you enjoy choosing new actors." Chase sipped his coffee, waiting for his bagel. "I get a hundred questions every hour from the newbies about eating, drinking, where to find the privies, what to do when they get hot in their costumes. When that's over, I get to help train a dozen new knights and one or two jousters for the Field of Honor."

"Poor Chase." Daisy stuck out her lower lip. "We all feel your pain, buddy. You also get to spend time with all the lovely young ladies who need a strong arm to get them through the day."

Bart laughed. "If you need any help with that, give me a call."

Daisy punched him hard in the shoulder, but it would've taken a lot more for her to hurt him. Bart was a giant of a man, close to seven feet tall, with crazy black hair that always looked as though he'd just removed a helmet. He could lift me straight off the ground. I'd seen him pick up two troublemakers at the same time, one under each arm. He made Chase look fragile.

Chase was tall and muscular—6'8", 250 pounds of muscle—usually wrapped in tight brown leather. He wore his long brown hair in a braid and had a gold pirate ring in one ear. His soulful brown eyes showed his intelligence and patience.

When he wasn't working as Chief of Security for the Village in his job as Bailiff, he worked on his own as a consulting patent attorney. He was very good with horses and had started at the Village in the jousting arena. I've never seen a man who looked better in armor.

And he was mine!

"I like all the unusual characters that people try out." I slid my arm through Chase's and rested my hand on his so that our matching wedding bands were together. Sometimes I just liked to remind myself that we were really a couple now. We'd finally gotten married and were living our happily ever after.

"Yeah." Daisy grinned. "Remember that woman last August who had the really tall hair that kept falling off?"

Bart laughed. "She was extremely funny."

Chase shrugged. "Really funny when I had to close the Good Luck fountain because her hair fell into it and really disgusting picking that up."

"You need to delegate more," Daisy said. "Tell him, Jessie. He does too much and doesn't make the rest of his security people do anything."

"I tell him that every day. Sometimes three times a day. He won't listen."

Chase's radio buzzed. It kept him in touch with the rest of the security guards as they tried to keep the Village running smoothly. "And it starts. The Main Gate is open, and already one of the new actors rode a horse through the Village Green."

He got up to leave. I tried to stop him. "Let someone else handle it. You have a hundred security guards. One of them can tell the person they can't have a real horse here."

Chase slid his hand into my short, brown hair and kissed me. Then he grabbed his bagel. "This is my job. You know that. Love you. See you later."

It was only a few moments after he was gone that we heard someone running through the Village calling out unsettling news.

"Princess Isabelle is dead! Oh tidings of great sorrow! Princess Isabelle is dead!"

Chapter Two

Daisy, Bart, and I only made it into the castle a few seconds before it was closed to the public. We were following Chase. Gus, the Master-at-Arms and gatekeeper, wasn't at his post, so security people were there to keep everyone out.

I wondered about Gus. I'd never seen him gone from his post regardless of weather or time of day. It was odd. Did Chase know where he was?

A sizable group of Village residents had gathered as they'd heard the news. Chase and his security guards tried to keep everyone out, but the cobblestones were crowded with new actors, thousands of visitors to the Village, and hundreds of residents who lived there. It wasn't an easy task.

Residents of the castle were standing in the walled garden that was favored by the royalty. All of Isabelle's retinue were there, weeping and wailing. King Harold and Queen Olivia were also present, standing close together and whispering between each other. Rita Martinez, head of the kitchen staff, was standing near the garden wall, her expression blank. Sir Reginald was squatting close to Isabelle's body.

Chase had just entered the garden after helping to set up the perimeter. He silently scanned the area around Isabelle. "What happened?" he asked the people around him.

Rita wiped her eyes. "I was walking out of the castle for a cigarette break. She was already here."

"Did you see anyone else out here?" he questioned.

"No. Just poor Isabelle. It was terrible." She hid her face in her hands.

"Anyone else?" Chase looked around at the familiar faces.

"She liked to dance up there," one of Isabelle's ladies (the one with the perfume from the museum) recounted. "Her terrace is right above us. She must have slipped and fallen."

"Where were all of you when this happened?" Chase knew royal personages were rarely alone.

"We were doing her bidding." The girl with the parasol from that morning said. "Her clothes needed washing. Her hairdresser was coming today. Her shoes needed brushing."

As she said shoes, I noticed Isabelle's dainty feet. They were encased in the dancing slippers Bill was making for her.

That meant Bill had been there. My heart started pumping harder. Where was he when Isabelle fell off the terrace?

Where is he now?

The sound of sirens entering the Village meant that Detective Almond and his officers had arrived. His group from the Myrtle Beach Police Department handled problems Chase and his people couldn't take care of.

It was a good time to look for Bill—before Chase or the police noticed that he'd been there and started asking questions we didn't have answers for yet.

I cautiously walked away, taking a sharp right and going into the castle. Bill could still be in Isabelle's suite, or somewhere in the castle. It wouldn't be a good thing if he'd been the last person to see her alive. It would only be a matter of time before someone grieving for her would remember that he'd been there to fit the slippers.

I hoped this wasn't a result of Isabelle reverting to her true nature and rebuffing Bill's advances. Not that I thought Bill would actually hurt her. I hadn't known him long, but he seemed like a wonderful, gentle soul. If there had been an accident, not really his fault, the sooner it was cleared up the better.

There was a side door from the garden that led to a secret passage. Once in the passage, I could go anywhere inside. Because I'd worked in the castle for a few summers, I knew my way around. I ran up the stone walkway to Isabelle's chambers. But the rooms were empty.

I checked the heavy, iron terrace railing, peeking over it. Detective Almond was already in the garden talking with Chase and all the castle dwellers that were there.

But no sign of Bill. I didn't know if that was good or bad.

Was it possible Isabelle had slipped and fallen even though the railing around the terrace was still intact?

Probably not. She would have had to cartwheel across the railing.

Someone could have picked her up and thrown her over. Someone large and strong. Not even that large and strong, really. Isabelle was tiny. She might have weighed 90 pounds, but no more.

I thought it could have been suicide, but whatever Isabelle would have used to climb over the rail would still be there. She wasn't tall enough to step over it, even with magic slippers.

I kind of snooped around her luxurious quarters. There were thick, expensive rugs on the stone floor and colorful unicorn-filled tapestries on the walls. Her bed was on a raised dais with heavy, pink velvet curtains surrounding it. The bathroom was spacious and also pink with a tub that could easily accommodate at least three people.

The other room was a big sitting area with a large screen television hanging on one wall, and a fireplace on another. Her windows were floor-length and faced the terrace on the sunny side of the castle.

I snooped through her closet. It was stuffed full of dresses and shoes. There was a lovely purple velvet cape I wouldn't have said no to. I realized it was a little inappropriate to ogle her clothes with her dying recently. I shut the closet door and started to leave the bedroom.

Then I heard Detective Almond's voice. The man only had two audio settings, loud and louder. He and Chase were walking into the suite. It was my cue to leave.

But with the two men coming in the doorway, I had to be creative or answer uncomfortable questions. The passage that had led me here connected every room in the castle to every other room. It made it easier and more discreet when the staff needed to bring something—or someone—in without being seen.

The passage from Isabelle's suite was located behind a bookcase. I pulled the lever, and the bookcase swung silently open. I scooted into the passage and closed it behind me.

The passages between castle rooms weren't dark or dusty like the ones in scary movies. Because they were used so frequently by everyone from the king and queen down to the lowliest servant, they were cleaned with the rest of the castle each day. Electric lights in sconces were always on so that no one got lost. It was easy to find my way to the kitchen area.

Everyone in the castle knew about the passageways. It would be possible for anyone to have killed Isabelle and escape without being seen by her retinue.

I was only speculating and also laying groundwork in my mind in case Bill was accused of having something to do with Isabelle's death. He was new to the Village. He'd never worked in the castle. He would have had to go in and out through the suite door. Everyone would have seen him.

Once I reached the kitchen, I ran outside. I was surprised

Rita had taken her cigarette break in the garden rather than the courtyard. The kitchen courtyard was where all the castle employees congregated on their breaks. The garden was more for the royal personages and their guests.

What was she doing there?

It was as much a mystery as Gus's absence from the gate.

I could use all of these things to help Bill—if he needed it. I hoped he wouldn't, but weird things happened sometimes. I knew that better than most.

But what if Bill was responsible for what happened to Isabelle?

I had to consider that idea too. I'd been so ready to defend him from false accusations, but what if he killed Isabelle?

No. I didn't believe it. I was a pretty good judge of character. Bill was no killer—I'd wager my new sandals on it.

Still a thought once considered can never be un-thought. Worry niggled at the edge of my awareness. I'd brought Bill to the Village. If he killed Isabelle, I was partially responsible.

Police officers were standing guard at the garden, probably waiting for the medical examiner. More people were coming from the Village to see what was going on but weren't able to get through Chase's security.

Going out of the area wasn't a problem. I grabbed a basket of flowers someone had left on the ground and walked out quickly. I needed to find Bill. I hoped he wasn't involved in this, but the sooner we started asking questions, the better.

Maybe this all sounds a little heartless considering that Isabelle was dead. I felt bad about it – really. I wasn't laughing about her death, but I wasn't crying either. She would have felt the same about me, if our positions had been reversed.

I was also hoping she wouldn't come back as a ghost like Wanda.

I started checking all the usual places Bill liked to hang out between working on the exhibit. Where would he have gone after dropping off Isabelle's slippers? I knew he enjoyed the taverns and pubs scattered throughout the Village. It seemed doubtful that he would've gone back to the tiny housing space he shared with Fred. He'd complained about it enough that I knew he wasn't happy there. Maybe he went to his stall or to the museum.

I wasn't surprised to see visitors leaving the Village with haste and deliberation. Several uniformed police officers, and security guards, were herding them toward the Main Gate. Detective Almond had apparently decided to close the Village early for the investigation. No doubt it would be less confusing to deal only with the residents.

But what if one of the visitors had killed Isabelle? He must not have thought of that. He was already sure it was an inside job.

I had to find my cobbler.

Mary, Mary Quite Contrary was taking off her blond wig as she headed home. William Shakespeare was still packing up his writing supplies from his podium. King Arthur had Excalibur slung across his back. He pulled the sword from the stone several times each day.

I saw my assistant, Manawydan Argall, showing his resident pass to a police officer at the gate. I was so glad to see him. Maintenance men were hanging the new banner on the museum announcing Bill's debut tomorrow. I hoped it would still happen.

"I'm so glad you're here!" I hugged Manny. "I missed you. Did you have a good vacation?"

"It's wonderful to be back." He was dressed, as always, in Victorian garb rather than something from the Middle Ages. But with all the steampunk elements coming into the Village, it didn't seem so out of place anymore. He was always particularly neat and clean and smelled of fresh air and flowers.

"How was it at home?"

Manny was from a small kingdom in Africa where he was the crown prince, as wild as that sounded.

"It was odd after being gone for so long. I kept expecting storybook characters to go in and out of the mansion each day. There were elephants trumpeting during the night, however, so I felt at ease. How is the cobbler exhibit progressing?"

"Thank you for knowing that you don't have to eat a cobbler." I laughed and hugged him again. He was so much more than just my assistant. We'd become good friends. "I'm still hearing jokes about it."

"People find the oddest things humorous here," he remarked. "On my way in, I saw a woman dressed as a spider. Everyone was laughing and taking pictures of her."

"It's the week we take on new actors for the Village." We walked toward the museum. "You're going to see all kinds of strange costumes and acts."

He adjusted his large glasses. "As though that doesn't happen every day here, Lady Jessie. Where is everyone going?"

"We may have a problem with the cobbler." I told him quickly about Princess Isabelle and my belief that Bill had been at the castle.

His dark eyes widened. "Magic from elves? Can this be true?"

Manny was a little naïve after spending years out of touch with the world. Growing up as a prince was isolating. He'd had to run away from home to experience the world without the royal cotton batting his parents had used to protect him.

"I doubt it—though anything is possible. He believes it."

The Big Bad Wolf joined us. The costume was hot so he'd removed the headpiece. "I s'pose you two know about Isabelle?"

"We know."

"It's a tragedy." Manny sighed. "She was so beautiful."

The new bookstore and print shop owner, Paul Samuels,

gave us each a single sheet of paper. His shop was called Rare Books. "Have you seen the latest issue? It's the first edition of my Village newspaper."

The wolf examined it closely, perhaps needing spectacles. "Princess Isabelle murdered by Shoemaker? What shoemaker?"

Manny stared at me. "Is that true?"

"No. Of course not. Bill didn't murder anyone."

Paul grinned. "People saw him with her only moments before she died. It's a scoop!"

"My good man," Manny advised. "Scoop is not the proper term for this news, not here at the Village. I'm not sure what would be. You should consult a historian."

"I think scoop is okay," the wolf said. "What do you think, Jessie?"

"I think I have to find Bill. I'll talk to you later." I continued on my path. There was no one at the museum. Bill's stall was closed.

"Wait for me!" Manny was huffing along behind me. "Do you think something happened between Isabelle and Bill?"

"I don't know yet. I have to talk to him. He's going to be a perfect suspect if Detective Almond decides to call Isabelle's death a murder." I changed course and headed for Peter's Pub. I had to find Bill and talk to him before the rumors got any worse—and to assure myself that everything was okay with him.

"I'll be happy to be of assistance. I could take the pubs on the left side of the Village, and you could take the pubs on the right."

"Thanks. Sorry to get you caught up in everything right away before you even have a chance to settle in." He was still holding the canvas bag he'd traveled with. He had to be the least prince-like person in the world. Our Village royalty could learn a few things from him.

He smiled. "It feels like home now, Lady Jessie. What would the Village be without a bit of intrigue and the aroma of roasted turkey legs in the air?"

"Okay. If you find Bill, let me know. We can use our cell phones since the Village is closed. I'll stop by the Dungeon and get mine."

He frowned. "I did not buy a cell phone while I was gone. I'm sorry. It simply seemed impractical since we can barely use them here."

"All right." I thought about it. "There's bound to be someone you can send to find me. Or bring Bill with you. Just don't let him out of your sight!"

He made a beautiful bow. "Your servant!"

I was happy with that plan since it meant I wouldn't have to check for Bill at the Lady in the Lake Tavern. The new owner and I had a few hard feelings between us. I avoided it like yesterday's mutton.

Manny and I separated, and I went into Peter's Pub.

The tavern and eatery was crowded with residents—it was half-price drink night besides the Village closing early. There was bound to be a ton of free food left over. Many of the pubs and restaurants would welcome hungry residents.

Peter Greenwalt hailed me and set up a tankard of ale. He was the owner of Peter's Pub. "Will Chase be joining you?"

"Probably not." I tried to scan the interior of the pub without being obvious about it. "He's busy with Princess Isabelle's death."

Peter's broad face lost color. "I hadn't heard. That's a terrible thing. Princess Isabelle was the jewel of the castle."

I tried to hide my skepticism at his remark. I wasn't as successful with my words. "Really? I don't know anyone who felt like that about her, except people who didn't know her well. I think the two of you knew each other very well."

He blushed down to the roots of his brown muttonchops and beard. "That was a long time ago between me and Isabelle. She really was a good woman—at heart."

I knew that he and Isabelle had once had a thing. It was over before I was at the Village all the time, but gossip had a way of continuing. "It's okay, Peter. If every man in the Village who slept with Isabelle is questioned about her death, the police will be here all month! I know you didn't have anything to do with it. Have you seen Bill Warren?"

"You mean the new shoemaker?" He used a large white cloth to wipe the glossy wood bar. "Not recently. He was here after lunch. Tomorrow's his big day, huh? Think he bugged out because he was nervous?"

He obviously hadn't heard the rumor about Bill killing Isabelle yet.

"Yeah. That's probably it. Thanks. I'll talk to you later." I drank down the ale he'd so kindly poured for me and walked quickly out of the pub.

I knew the next place on my side of the Village was the Pleasant Pheasant where Chase and I mostly hung out. It was close to the Dungeon where we lived. They served leftover food and drinks into the night. Residents ate for free many times.

There was only coffee at the Monastery Bakery or tea at the Honey and Herb Shoppe between Peter's and the Pleasant Pheasant. Bill liked something stronger.

Manny had definitely taken on the bulk of possibilities of where Bill could be hanging out. At the other side of the Village was not only the Lady in the Lake Tavern, but also Baron's Beer and Brats, Peasant's Pub, and Brewster's.

I decided not to feel too bad about the disparity. Manny had just come back from vacation.

I walked past the Dutchman's Stage where a few comedians were still practicing. Luke Helms, the owner of the Jolly Pipe Maker's Shop, was sitting on his steps, working on a handful of new pipes. The scent of his tobacco floated through the air.

"Good evening to you, Lady Jessie." He tugged at his cap. His silver-colored glasses glinted in the light from his shop window. "Thought I'd sit out on this lovely evening. It's too hot to sit inside."

"It is indeed, sir. Have you seen the new shoemaker?"

"You mean Bill?" He squinted up at me. "Certainly. He was here earlier. We shared a few pints, and he said he had to go."

"Did he mention where he was going?"

Luke put down the pipe he was carving. "Is something wrong?"

"Not at all. Just a few last minute things for the museum opening tomorrow."

He smiled. "Wish you'd have me at the museum sometime, Lady Jessie. My work could use a kick in the pants. People just don't smoke pipes like they used to, you know? Maybe if you run out of artists, you could have me up there."

"You are an artist, Luke. And I'll find a date for you to show your pipes at the museum."

He grinned. "Thank you. Have you heard the news about Princess Isabelle? That new fella from the bookstore says she was murdered. I can't imagine who would want to kill her. She was the sweetest thing ever. She'll be missed, she will."

I jumped as I felt a strong arm go around my waist. "I have to borrow my wife for a moment, Luke. Have a good evening."

"You too, Bailiff. Good luck catching that killer." Luke saluted him.

Chase started walking away, taking me with him. "I saw you at the castle, you know. Where's Bill?"

"I don't know. I was looking for him. It's like everyone has seen him, just not recently. Why are you looking for him?"

"Pretty sure we're looking for him for the same reason. It sounds like he was the last one to see Isabelle alive."

"Bill didn't kill Isabelle," I told him. "Maybe she killed herself."

"Detective Almond doesn't think that's the case since she was thrown an extra twenty feet over what she could have jumped from the terrace. I'm sure you know that too."

"How would I know? I leave that stuff to you and

Detective Almond."

He laughed. "Sure you do. Where's Bill?"

"I don't know. That's why I'm looking for him."

"Because you know he was with Isabelle?"

"No. Although even if he was with her, that doesn't mean he killed her. I admit that I don't know him very well, but what I know of him, he seems harmless. He's always good-natured, and he works very hard."

"Let's go back to the part where you don't know him that well. He's only been here about a month." Chase stopped walking and stared at me. "Where do you think he might be? Detective Almond isn't necessarily going to arrest him. He just wants to talk to him."

"You know Detective Almond always takes the first available suspect. I don't want that to be Bill. What about all the other residents of the Village who disliked her?"

"Like who? Everyone loved Isabelle."

It was my turn to laugh. "Only if you're a man. I don't know any women who even liked Isabelle, much less loved her. She took Adora's knight last year. She made a play for one of the Three Chocolatiers. She even went after Bawdy Betty's boyfriend. There were more than a few women who wouldn't have minded killing her."

I didn't mention myself because I didn't want him to know she bothered me that much.

"It had to be someone who was strong enough to pick her up and toss her over the rail," Chase explained. "I suppose I could think of a few men who weren't happy after she broke up with them. I can't think of any women strong enough to lift her, except maybe Daisy, but I don't think she and Isabelle ever had a run-in."

"All right. That's a place to start anyway. At least you're willing to admit it could be someone besides Bill."

"Except that he was probably the last one with her before she died. Three or four of her retinue saw him with her at the castle when he delivered her slippers. Maybe he had nothing to do with her death. But he might have seen something that can help Detective Almond find out who did kill her."

"Manny and I have been searching the pubs." I gave up trying to stall him. He was only trying to do his job. "Bill likes visiting the pubs and having a few ales. Manny is on the other side of the Village. I've already been through Peter's Pub. Luke said he was at the pipe shop until he ran out of ale. I'm headed for the Pleasant Pheasant."

"See?" He grinned, sliding his arm around me again. "That wasn't so hard. I'll come with you in case you find him. I'd like for Detective Almond to question Bill tonight, if he can. We can get this entire preliminary investigation over while the Village is closed. We don't want to drag it into tomorrow and risk being shut down again."

"All right." We walked past the tree swing and the privies that were near the Dungeon. I could hear laughter and music coming from Stage Caravan. Maybe someone there had seen Bill. "Let's try the stage. It sounds like a party. There's bound to be booze."

"I'm with you."

It was starting to get dark. Tiny fairy lights were coming on around the Village. There were two large stadium lights in the Village Square that were sometimes turned on for maintenance but not tonight. Every restaurant and shop had candle-like electric lights glowing from their windows.

There was electric lighting, and other modern conveniences in the apartments and shops. Everyone tried to use them only when the Village was closed. We loved our homes and wanted to preserve the ambiance of the Renaissance as much as we could.

Stage Caravan knew how to throw a party. There were huge torches burning at the four corners of the stage. I could smell the tequila before we got to the bar. A big banner had been hung to mourn the loss of one of the dancers who was leaving the Village—Bye-Bye Sheena! The party was in full swing with the male and female dancers in skimpy clothes grinding and shaking to the pulsing strains of exotic music.

The regular stage musicians were enjoying themselves with a few other musicians from around the Village.

I asked a few of the dancers if they'd seen Bill. Most of them didn't know who I was talking about. There were hundreds of residents in the Village. One man could easily go unnoticed for a few weeks. Bill was new and didn't have many relationships yet.

"Anything?" Chase asked as we met again at the side of the stage.

"No. Lots of tequila and fruit, but no sign of Bill."

"Other ideas? You know him a lot better than I do, Jessie."

Manny came riding up on one of the tall bikes from Simon's Spokes, the new bicycle shop. The bike was at least six feet high, a masterpiece of ingenuity. "I located him! He's at Brewster's, deep in the middle of a dart game. I asked Merlin to keep him there until our return."

There wasn't much I could say. I'd wanted Manny to keep an eye on Bill so we could keep this quiet. Merlin was the Village wizard who lived and worked at the apothecary shop near the castle. But he was also the CEO of Adventureland. He'd certainly have an interest in Bill—and in Isabelle's death.

"Don't worry, Lady Jessie," Manny assured me. "I told the wizard that you needed the cobbler to complete a project before the museum opened tomorrow. I don't think word of Isabelle's death has reached those at the tavern yet."

Manny was relatively new, too. He didn't realize that everyone would know about Isabelle, and about Bill's visit to her. There were probably already wagers on his guilt or innocence.

"There's nothing you can do to protect him now," Chase added, making it worse. "Let's get him over to the castle while Detective Almond is still here. Where's your belief in the system, Jessie?"

"I don't have one. Let's go."

We walked quickly across the King's Highway as

Manny tried to keep his seat on the tall bike.

"This is wonderful," he exclaimed as he almost lost his balance. "I want to purchase one of these. It would be so much better than walking all the time."

"I guess King Harry was right," Chase said. "Everyone else hates the bike shop rentals, but they'll probably be popular."

We passed Roger Trent from the Glass Gryphon. He was standing on the cobblestones talking with William Shakespeare. As soon as he saw Chase, Roger said goodnight to Shakespeare and quickly fell in with us.

"You're after Princess Isabelle's killer, I presume?" Roger was an ex-police officer who had been Village Bailiff before Chase. He still liked to take part in any chaos that occurred. He was a stocky, muscled man who worked out regularly. It was hard to imagine him as a cop, looking at his Village clothes of blue cotton shirt and black britches.

"Just asking questions and interviewing people to find out who saw what," Chase said.

"I've heard a few rumors." Roger glanced at me. I knew what he was going to say. "Some people say Bill Warren, the new shoemaker, was with Isabelle when she died."

Chase shook his head and kept walking. "We haven't confirmed that yet. We're talking to him—and several other people from Isabelle's retinue at the castle. Bill may not have been the last one to see her alive."

"You're not trying to protect him for Jessie's sake because his new exhibit starts tomorrow at the museum, are you? No offense."

"None taken." Chase gazed down at Roger, at least a head taller than him. "We have to talk to everyone. You know that."

"I'm taking offense at that," I told Roger. "Chase wouldn't look the other way for something so serious. He's been Bailiff a long time. How long are you going to pester him because he took your job away?"

"Pester him? Chase wouldn't have been able to solve

half the problems he has without my help." Roger glared at me.

"I suppose I could say the same thing. So could Detective Almond. But we're not jealous of him." I glared right back at him.

"Jessie," Chase said. "Not now. Let's stay focused. If Roger can add to the investigation, that's what's important."

Manny took a spill off the bike as we reached Brewster's. The lights were bright coming from inside the tavern. Laughter rushed out into the evening as Chase opened the door.

I helped Manny off the ground and brushed off his dusty tailcoat. He was unhurt but voicing a few drawbacks to riding the tall bike now that he'd tried it. We followed Roger and Chase inside where the dart tournament was still going strong.

I quickly scanned the crowded room. There were dozens of men and women with pints of beer in their hands, but no sign of Bill. Chase nodded at Merlin who stood in one corner wearing his signature purple, starred robe and pointed hat. We pushed through the crowd to reach him.

"Where's Bill?" Chase asked him.

Merlin cupped a hand to his ear at another bout of raucous laughter. "What? What's wrong, Bailiff? Have you located Princess Isabelle's killer yet?"

"We're looking for the shoemaker," Roger yelled. "He's supposed to be here with you."

"Oh, you mean the cobbler?" Merlin pointed to the area where the dartboard hung. "Over there. But you can't have him yet. I have twenty dollars on his nose."

I looked back and saw Bill acting as a human dartboard. There was a line of half-drunk people waiting to throw darts at him.

"Stop!" I yelled, horrified. "What are you doing? He could be seriously hurt."

"Nah." Galileo offered his opinion. "He has elf magic. He can't be hurt. Ask him."

Merlin laughed. "I don't believe a word of it. I know magic, and he doesn't have any. I think someone will catch him in the nose. So far, no one has managed to hit him."

"Probably too drunk," Manny declared in a disgusted tone.

"We have to stop this," I said to Chase. "Blow a whistle or something to get their attention."

Roger climbed up on one of the crude wood tables and shouted for the tournament to stop. Either everyone ignored him or couldn't hear him—I wasn't sure which. I plunged into the crowd to keep the tournament from continuing, but I was too late.

Sam Di Vinci threw the next dart. It whizzed toward its goal, but suddenly went off-course and completely missed Bill's face.

"See?" Bill asked drunkenly. "Nothing bad can happen to me. Try again."

Everyone in the room was so tightly focused and closely pressed together where my cobbler stood, I couldn't push through them. I yelled out, "Bill, no!"

Another dart was immediately thrown by Master Archer Simmons who owned The Feathered Shaft archery shop. Cheers followed. I closed my eyes, knowing he wouldn't miss his target. When I heard laughter instead of groaning, I opened them again to find Bill still untouched.

I tried again to push my way through the crowd. There were just too many people. I looked up as Chase rammed his path through the group and positioned himself in front of Bill. That made my heart pound faster.

"That's it," Chase said loudly. "It's over. No more human targets. Everyone go home and get some sleep."

What he didn't see was that Mother Goose was next in line to throw her dart. She'd already flung the dart into the space between her and Chase before she could react to his pronouncement. It was headed directly for his eye. I screamed a warning to him and tried to get my hand in front of it.

The tight-knit group groaned. Some covered their eyes. Mother Goose fainted dead away on the tavern floor. Bill gestured with one hand. The dart veered to the right, missing him and Chase, embedding itself in the wall beside them.

Mother Goose sat up and shrieked, her large gray mobcap falling from her short white hair. "Oh my God! What in the world were you thinking, Sir Bailiff? I could have put out your eye."

"Exactly why you shouldn't have been throwing darts at the shoemaker," Chase told her in an angry voice he rarely used. "Get your goose and go home. We'll discuss this tomorrow."

"But it's different with Bill," Mother Goose argued. "He has elf magic. We couldn't hit him with a dart. He said so."

"Never mind that." Roger took charge of the crowd. Phineas the goose squawked as he lifted him and gave him to Mother Goose. "You heard the Bailiff. Everyone out of the tavern. Go home."

I rushed to Bill and Chase's sides. "Are you all right? How could you do something so crazy?"

The question was addressed as much to Chase as it was to Bill.

Bill finished his beer in a gulp. "You don't have to worry about me, Lady Jessie. I'm the only one who can do something bad to myself. No one else can hurt me."

"You're drunk," Chase said. "What are you talking about?"

"I killed Princess Isabelle. I'll have to spend the rest of my life in prison. I'd say that's about as bad as it gets."

Chapter Three

I walked with Bill to the castle even though Chase assured me that it wasn't necessary. "You're not his lawyer, Jessie. There's nothing you can do for him."

"I'm his friend," I responded. "There's no law against me being with him." I lowered my voice. Bill was right ahead of us. "Besides, I don't believe he killed Isabelle."

"He confessed."

"He's drunk and probably upset because Isabelle showed him the door as soon as she got her slippers. He was way out of his league with her."

"Isabelle was single and available. There wasn't any reason for her not to date as many men as she pleased," he defended her.

"That's true, but she left a string of broken hearts behind her too. Any one of those people could have pushed her over the rail."

"Let's talk about this later," Chase growled as he saw Detective Almond approaching us.

Chase had called the police detective about Bill's confession before we left Brewster's.

That call allowed Detective Almond to be almost jovial when we met him. "Well, well! I like a case that wraps up quickly."

"Me too," Chase agreed.

"Good work, Manhattan! You're becoming a fine detective. You could always come to work for us at MBPD, if you decide you want a normal job."

"Thanks."

Everyone that had been kicked out of Brewster's, along with another fifty or so residents of the Village, waited to hear what was happening.

Bill stretched out his arms to the police officers who'd accompanied Detective Almond. He almost fell over in the process. "I've already admitted my wrongdoing. Take me in. I deserve to be punished for killing Princess Isabelle."

A lot of murmuring ran through the residents. We were close to Mirror Lake. A shot rang out from the pirate ship, Queen's Revenge. Sometimes the pirates practiced shooting off their cannons after the Village closed. It was enough to make a few people jump. The rest were annoyed.

"I understand that, Mr. Warren." Detective Almond moved closer to him. "I appreciate your cooperation in this matter. Thank you for making my job easier."

"I'm glad it's out in the open." Bill hung his head. "I didn't mean to hurt her. I'm sure we could've been lovers."

Someone close to me coughed as they muttered, "Yeah. Right."

I smiled triumphantly at Chase. I wasn't the only one who felt that way about Isabelle.

"Let's finish this conversation downtown." Detective Almond put his hand on Bill's shoulder, and they started walking.

"I wish I could renounce my elf magic." Bill spat the words as though he hated them.

Detective Almond stopped walking. "What are you

talking about?"

"I killed Isabelle with my elf magic. It was a mistake. Sometimes I make the shoes and they're out of control. I think they're imbued with too much magic, you see. I had to forcibly stop a man from trying to climb a lamp pole once because he was wearing my climbing boots—they were only for mountain climbing. He might have been injured or killed trying to get up that post, especially since the boots would climb anything."

Chase shook his head. Detective Almond glared at him in the dim light.

"So you're saying your shoes killed Isabelle Franklin?" Detective Almond's happy face was quickly disappearing into the disgusted expression he usually wore when he came to the Village.

"Yes." Bill wiped away a tear. "I made them too powerful, I guess. She danced right off the terrace. If she wouldn't have been up that high, she could've danced until she fell down, exhausted. I didn't reckon with when and where she'd put them on. I'm truly sorry."

I smiled—I knew Bill didn't kill Isabelle. He thought his slippers did, but that was nonsense—unless she'd jumped over the rail while she was dancing.

"Could I have a word with you, Bailiff?" Detective Almond called Chase outside the ever-growing group of residents.

"That doesn't sound like murder to me." Merlin voiced his opinion. "It would be the same with me if I cast a spell on someone and they died."

"Because you don't really have any magic either," I reminded him.

"But Bill has elf magic," Mother Goose said. "He should be somewhat responsible for that, don't you think?"

Roger huffed. "Don't be absurd. There's no such thing as elf, or any other kind of magic. Either the guy killed her or he didn't. Shoes don't kill people. The Bailiff should know better."

I agreed with Roger for once. Except for the part about Chase. Bill hadn't told us everything. There was no way to know that he believed his shoes had killed Isabelle when we'd left Brewster's.

"I've seen him use his magic," Phil Ferguson from the Sword Spotte said. "Tonight he made a tankard of ale completely disappear."

"He probably drank it, you idiot." Roger shook his head. "I'm going home."

The coming of magic to the Village had definitely upset the fine line between fact and fiction that we all walked each day. Now no one was sure where the precarious line was that separated the two worlds. Some people believed—some didn't.

I was still on the line.

Chase came back after exchanging words with Detective Almond. "He still wants to take Bill in for questioning. He thinks he might be confessing but using the magic thing as an insanity defense."

"You mean he doesn't believe I have elf magic?" The expression on Bill's face was one of complete amazement.

"No. He doesn't believe in magic," Chase told him as two officers came to escort Bill to a car. "But maybe you can convince him. You're going to spend some quality time with him for the next few hours."

Bill stared at me. "I've never lied about my magic. I can't understand why he doesn't believe me."

"Just go with them for now," I said. "Don't worry about a thing. You just tell them the truth and everything will be fine."

"Do you really believe that, Lady Jessie?" Bill's eyes begged for an answer.

"No. Not really." I hadn't meant to say it out loud. I retrenched. "I don't think you killed Isabelle. Do the best you can tonight. Chase will get you out tomorrow if he needs to." I hugged him before the officers started walking away him.

"Why did you tell him I'd get him out?" Chase asked.

"You know I don't practice that kind of law."

"You can bail him out if they charge him," I reminded him. "But I'm telling you–Bill didn't kill Isabelle."

"Why are you so certain, Jessie?"

"Magic?"

He frowned. "That's what I thought."

There were some heavy sighs from the people around us. Merlin declared that he was going home. Phil Ferguson patted Chase on the back before he left.

Fred the Red Dragon, wearing only the bottom of his costume, wished us both goodnight and asked if Bill going with the police meant he could have his house back to himself.

"I'm sure Bill will be back tomorrow," I answered. "Don't get too comfortable."

Chase and I started back toward the Dungeon. "I can't believe Bill thinks he killed Isabelle with magic shoes," he said.

"I think he really believes the elf magic thing. He takes it very seriously."

We walked past the quiet eateries of Polo's Pasta and Three Pigs Barbecue. I could smell the smoky barbecue being readied for tomorrow. The Village Green was quiet as we shuffled through the lush green grass in the middle of the King's Highway.

"Do you believe it, Jessie?" Chase asked me.

"I don't know. If you'd asked me that question five years ago, I would've said no." I glanced up at the stars. "Now, after our crazy wedding, and Wanda's ghost—not to mention the sorcerer and Tilly Morgenstern—I'm not so positive about it."

"I know what you mean." He put his arm around me as we walked. "What about me? Do you still believe in me?"

"What do you mean? I know you're real." I pinched his arm and smiled as he yelped.

"I mean do you still believe that I love you?"

"Of course I do. Why are you asking?"

He glanced away and then grinned before he kissed me. "Just thinking about what you said about Isabelle. You know, most of that was rumors and gossip. She wasn't as bad as people made her sound."

"You knew her better than me, I guess." Yes, Isabelle had dated Chase before I came along. She'd always claimed that I'd stolen him from her. What was he getting at?

"You know everyone here loves a good story. The story doesn't have to be true."

"I know that everyone loves to gossip, Chase. Are you worried about something they could be saying about us?"

"No," he denied.

But I wasn't sure I believed him and I had a hard time getting to sleep that night.

Chapter Four

Chase left early the next morning to find out what had happened to Bill. We'd expected him back during the night, but no one had knocked on our door.

I wanted to go but had to stay to get everything set up for the exhibit. King Harold had sent a messenger to let me know that he wanted the museum to open with the shoe exhibit anyway, even if Bill didn't come back. They'd spent too much money on advertising for the event. Visitors would see his work and his methods, the messenger had droned. Manny and I were to come up with a plan to escort visitors through the museum and describe how a shoemaker worked during the Renaissance.

That part wouldn't be too hard since I'd done my homework so I could answer questions during the exhibit. The hard part was going to be explaining while all the banners and ads said we were going to have a real, live shoemaker, but he wasn't there.

The Village opened at ten a.m. like always. The

cobblestone walkway that circled the Village was crowded with new and strange actors. I immediately noticed a man dressed like a llama who only talked with his puppet hand.

Yeah. Like he was going to make it to day two.

There was also a woman with huge blue bird wings that flapped up and down as she walked. She called out in the most authentic bird voice I'd ever heard. I saw Lord Maximus, who runs the Hawk Stage with his birds of prey show, eyeing her with a look of distaste and envy.

She wouldn't make the cut either.

I looked at the little cloth-covered book they'd given each of the permanent shopkeepers and actors to write down which actors and characters they saw and liked during the day. I wrote a notation about bird woman and llama man. I probably didn't need to bother since they didn't have a chance, but I liked them.

People didn't realize that the best way to get on at the Village was to become one of the characters already there. People were always leaving—there had been three King Arthurs in the last six months. The weird and exotic wasn't necessarily what the Village was looking for.

The trio of musicians who were playing at the museum opening were very excited about being there, and the extra money promised them by Adventureland. We talked about the music they'd play.

Each of them had a different stringed instrument—cello, violin, and mandolin. They had a good sound together, and I thought they'd do a wonderful job. I hoped the gig would get them noticed by the management. The trio had no permanent place to play each day. They were moved from courtyard to gazebo to stall all over the Village.

I left them, feeling pleased with their music. I was headed toward the Honey and Herb Shoppe that had been tapped to provide refreshments for the event. Not that I had to worry about what Mrs. Potts, the owner, would do. But she could need help, and I was hoping she might have a few honey cookies fresh from the oven.

Before I could reach her shop, Wanda Le Fey—the resident ghost Bill and I had been talking about—joined me.

Wanda would be forever blue thanks to a packet of dye I'd put in her shower before she died. How did I know someone would be waiting to kill her when she got out? Her bright red hair streamed around her blue face with a life of its own, wind currents that I couldn't feel, blowing past her.

"Good morning, your ladyship." She was as British in life as shew as in death. She made an awkward curtsey. It didn't really matter since her feet didn't touch the ground.

Did I mention she was also completely naked? I guessed she'd be that way forever too.

"Wanda."

"What brings you out on this fine morning?"

"I'm working. What have you been up to?" I could see people passing me, staring at me as it appeared that I was talking to myself. Occasionally someone stared at Wanda, and I knew he or she could see her too. They probably wondered if Wanda was real or just an actor playing a floating, naked, blue woman.

"A little of this, and a little of that." She stretched her smile maliciously. "I frightened an entire group of children visiting from a daycare not five minutes ago. The little tikes ran hither and yon as their guardians tried to stop them. It was quite amusing."

"I'll bet it was. Why don't you try doing good things for a change? That might be fun too."

"Oh Jessie, you know I'm not made that way. I had the best times when I was a nurse here, wrapping bandages too tightly and making injections hurt. It's who I am. But I'm so much better now."

"You should hope one of those ghost hunter groups who come through to find you don't ever come with an exorcist. You might find yourself in a much worse place to haunt."

She laughed as she lifted her face to the morning sun. "I quite love my death, thank you." Then she turned her baleful, dead eyes on me. "But you aren't looking so happy this morning. Trouble in paradise with your Bailiff? I did warn you that marriage wouldn't be as sweet. You didn't listen. Now every young woman who goes to him for help will look like a way out of the trap you've put him in."

As she spoke, a group of attractive young women went by us in their thin, low-cut summer gowns. They smiled and flicked their parasols, the breezes from the Atlantic wafting through their silky hair.

Wow! Where did that come from?

"I'm not worried about Chase." I was thinking about what he'd said last night. Something was up. How could I not know what it was?

"Perhaps. But it makes sense to me. You'd better watch your step, sweetie. I won't be there to pick you up when you fall." She disappeared with a wild cackle of laughter.

I looked around. No one else seemed to hear it. There was a very nicely done gargoyle walking past me. He smiled and saluted, breaking character, but I didn't hold that against him. His makeup and costume were phenomenal.

The welcoming committee was at the Main Gate, singing and handing out maps of the Village. Robin Hood and a few of his Merry Men were there to help welcome the steady stream of visitors. Fred the Red Dragon was sending up small puffs of smoke, and the Tornado Twins—Diego and Lorenzo—were cracking jokes while they showed off their piglet that wore a skirt and hat. The flower girls smiled and tossed their petals at visitors as they entered.

There were always different people at the gate each morning and evening. The king and queen were insistent on smiling faces, flowers, and music welcoming their arriving and departing guests.

I saw another great costume. This one was a muscular, white-skinned angel with gossamer wings. It looked as though the man had only painted his naked body, with an appropriate white patch. That created a lot of giggling with the flower girls.

Beside him were two men dressed like different versions

of Dr. Who. The Village had become increasingly more steampunk in the last few years. I'd seen visitors dressed as the Tardifs. I didn't expect Dr. Who clones to make the cut, but I saw several steampunk characters with goggles and astrolabes coming in that might be interesting. This was an open casting call so anyone or anything could walk through the gate.

I could only tell the difference between the visitors and the actors trying out for parts because the actors wore red badges identifying themselves. Each actor also had a number on his badge for ease in scoring them.

Mrs. Potts was boxing up her fresh cookies and fruit bread when I arrived. She was wearing her usual bright blue dress and white mobcap, her ruddy face smiling. "Come in, Lady Jessie. Perhaps you can help me get all of this to the museum. That silly boy I hired seems to have overslept."

The sunshine streamed in from the windows creating a pleasant place to visit. Mrs. Potts never had to do much to have a roomful of visitors each day. I helped her box everything including real china teacups, saucers, and spoons.

"How is the new exhibit coming along?" she asked as we started across the street to the museum. "I'm so excited to be catering this event. No one ever thinks to ask me. They go to the King's Tarts or Bawdy Betty's Bagels. I'm sure everyone will be pleased with my treats."

"I know you're right." I bit into a cookie and rolled my eyes. "Everyone will want you to cater their special events after today. Your honey cookies are to die for."

"Speaking about dying—terrible news about Isabelle—though she probably deserved her untimely demise."

"I suppose so."

"And what of the shoemaker? Did he really kill her with magic shoes?"

"I don't think so. Bill is very nice and especially gifted. I think he fell in love with Princess Isabelle when he first met her. She was really nice to him too. I was surprised. I thought maybe they could have something, but then she died."

Mrs. Potts cleared her throat and adjusted her cap. She was probably in her sixties, but her portly body moved quickly as she avoided dozens of people on tall bicycles. "He goes that way, does he?" she asked in a slightly irritated tone.

"What do you mean?"

"I was hoping—since I knew he was an older gentleman—that he might be someone who could be interested in a well-preserved woman like myself. But if he's already sniffing at the young ones, there's no hope for me."

We were both a little out of breath by the time we'd made it through the growing crowd and climbed the museum stairs. I knew Mrs. Potts, despite her name, had never been married. "Bill is probably overwhelmed right now. You know how the Village does that to people. Who knows what he's really like?"

I realized that Mrs. Potts clearly needed my help. I was without a doubt the best matchmaker in the Village. Daisy and Bart were part of my legacy, as were Roger Trent from the Glass Gryphon and Mary Shift, the Gullah basket weaver from Wicked Weaves. Not to mention Daisy and Bart. I was sure I could help Mrs. Potts too. "Maybe you're right, Jessie." She studied me kindly as she regained her breath. "I hear you and Chase are having a few problems. It's not unusual when you're approaching your first year anniversary, you know."

Renaissance Village was a spectacular place to live and work, but it was a hotbed of gossip—some true and some not so true. Something was going on. I wasn't sure what yet, but rumors started from some small occurrences sometimes. I didn't like the idea that people were talking about Chase and me breaking up. I had to nip that rumor in the bud.

Yet I had to consider that Chase knew something about what was going on after last night's discussion.

"Chase and I are very happy together," I finally said. "I don't know what happened that caused this gossip, but it's all wrong. We're fine—outside of him taking his job too seriously maybe."

Mrs. Potts took my hand in her soft white one. "Do you think it's because he needs some time to himself away from home?"

"No! I don't think that. Chase has always been this way. You know what I'm talking about. He doesn't think anyone can do his job except him."

She sighed. "Denying a problem is not the way to solve it, Jessie. That's all I'm saying."

Argh! It was stupid to try to undo the rumor mill. I knew better. I'd only make it worse if I kept defending us. I was going to have to tough it out until something new and exciting caught everyone's fancy.

"Thank you, Mrs. Potts." I hoped everything was set up as our first visitors of the day began creeping in. "I appreciate you doing this today."

She smiled and glanced away. I knew what she was thinking. I wished I knew why she was thinking it.

First Wanda and then Mrs. Potts. The whole Village thought Chase and I were about to split up. It was irritating since there was no truth to it. It wouldn't be easy to get everyone to stop talking about it either. I'd just have to ignore it. But that was easier to say than do.

I almost ran into Manny as I headed toward Bill's work area. He had an alarmed expression on his face that had nothing to do with our near collision.

He grasped my hand in his. "Are you and the Bailiff splitting up?"

"Who told you that?"

"It was Lady Godiva as I walked past the gate this morning. I am so sorry about your marriage. I thought the two of you were perfect for one another." He squeezed my hand, his eyes filled with sympathy.

"It's not true. It's been misinterpreted, Manny. You know how these things happen here. Someone probably saw Chase with another woman and decided he was doing something he shouldn't. The next thing you know, our marriage is on the rocks."

He bowed deeply, a sign of respect. "Whatever you say, Lady Jessie. You know that I am always here for you."

I'd said all I was going to say until I could talk to Chase and figure out what had started this snowball rolling. "At least one of us needs to stay here with Bill's work all the time. We're going to say that he was called away. Don't get into any speculation about what happened to Isabelle."

* * *

Crowds of visitors flocked to the museum. Manny and I were barely prepared for them. Some of the potential new actors came too. There were fauns, satyrs, Greek gods, and some really tall dwarfs. Manny and I laughed at a few of them as we marked our impressions in the little book.

"I don't think Lord Maximus is going to like a man walking around the Village with his own eagle." Manny made a note of it. "And there are so many princesses. I don't believe there is room for all of them."

I agreed. "I liked some of the animal characters, like the half-lion man. His costume was amazing."

"I enjoyed the butterfly woman. She was very graceful and colorful. I would certainly recommend her."

Several Lady Godivas, and a few Lord Godivas, passed us as we welcomed everyone at the door. Their full-bodysuits ranged from massively covering them to barely decent. I saw a few older visitors blushing at some of the costumes and hurrying away.

They wouldn't make the cut. This wasn't that kind of Village!

It turned out to be a beautiful day. The weather was a little cooler after the recent storm. Even the humidity wasn't as bad. There had been several hurricane scares since June when the season began, but no one had left the Village because of them.

A dozen steampunk gentlemen and their ladies filed into the museum. Their costumes were perfect—a blend of

Victorian history and science fiction. They were disappointed when Bill wasn't there to make new shoes and boots for them. Not surprisingly, the rumor of his elf magic had started getting around. Who wouldn't want magic boots?

Some of the ladies and a few gentlemen settled for boots that Bill had already made. I knew he'd be pleased to see that he'd made some money that day. I hoped he'd be back soon with Chase, and that his confession about killing Isabelle would be in the past.

The new owner of the Lady in the Lake Tavern paid us a visit. I wished I could leave for a while and come back again when she was gone, but I hated to leave Manny with the crowd and no shoemaker.

Tilly Morgenstern had taken over the old Lady of the Lake Tavern after her sister, Ginny Stewart, had gone to prison. Tilly held me responsible for that event, and she'd made it clear since she'd arrived that she hated me and wanted to do something awful to me.

It had been a year since she'd arrived and nothing much had happened—except for a few threats and uncomfortable encounters between us. I had avoided that area of the Village since she'd come. I was surprised that she'd visit the museum when she knew that I was the director.

"There she is, now." Tilly's voice had the quality of a small child's. Her laughter was infectious. Many people found themselves laughing over something almost against their will and wondering later why they'd laughed at all.

Her thick white hair hung down to her waist in curls while her face was a crooked road map of wrinkles around her hard, dark eyes. "Just the woman I was hoping to see today. Good afternoon to you, Lady Jessie."

"And to you, Tilly Morgenstern." I decided to keep the conversation on a polite, Renaissance level. Visitors stood all around us listening to what we said. I didn't want an incident at the museum. This was my life now. It was important to me.

"I wanted to get your opinion on some wonderful new

sandals your fine cobbler is making for me. It seems he's not here, but I ask for your judgment nonetheless. What say you?"

I was completely aware of her constant companion, Leo, who was always close to her. He was as tall as Chase, but not as broad as Bart. His shaved head was tattooed, and his empty white eyes gazed blindly around him. To make matters worse, Tilly claimed he'd had his tongue cut out by pirates.

All together not a pleasant sight, and frightening to have around, knowing how she felt about me. I wasn't the only one in the Village who saw them as a witch and her zombie. We were all too scared to say it, but we thought it and kept it to ourselves. I certainly didn't want Chase going up against the pair.

"The sandals are quite remarkable." I studied the design for them as they lay on Bill's cutting table. "Master Warren has done a wonderful job of creating them."

"Yes. That is exactly what I thought as well. Thank you, Lady Jessie." Tilly grinned, showing sharp white teeth. "Perhaps you and I might have a word in private."

Manny was standing behind Leo where I could see him, but Tilly couldn't without looking away from me. He was frantically shaking his head and waving his arms as he silently mouthed the word no over and over again. He knew about Tilly's threats against me.

But what could I say? I couldn't tell her I wouldn't speak to her—that would be inviting further reprisal when I kept hoping she might soften her stance against me. We both lived in the Village. If we couldn't be friends, I at least hoped we wouldn't be enemies.

I curtsied slightly, showing respect but without the sincerity that a deeper curtsy would convey. "Of course. Please step back here."

It was unlikely that she'd try to kill me in my own museum, right?

Chapter Five

Tilly followed me into one of the secondary rooms of the museum. All around us were historical artifacts, documents, and pictures of shoemaking. They'd taken me months to collect for the exhibit. Some were on loan from other museums.

Surprisingly, Tilly made a hand gesture as Leo started to follow her. He nodded and stayed where he was.

I gulped, and Manny's eyes got wide. Maybe Leo was blind, but he could certainly tell his mistress's wishes. It was part of what was creating their reputation in the Village.

"My dear," Tilly began as she studied the pictures on the wall. "I am also here to offer my services. I hear that you and the Bailiff are having some problems of a personal nature."

I took a deep breath. It was bad enough getting offers of help from my friends over an imaginary fight between me and my husband. It was far worse talking about it with Tilly, who I'd come to think of as my enemy.

"I assure you, Madame, that the Bailiff and I are not

having any problems of a personal, or any other sort of nature. I don't know what services you're referring to, but please don't trouble yourself on my behalf."

She smiled in a predatory way and shrugged her bony shoulders. Her diamond-hard eyes stared through me. "They say some wives are the last to know. I never took you for a fool, Lady Jessie. But if you learn the truth, and are looking for a spell to bring back a wandering husband, please know that my magic is always available to you."

Tilly having magic—some kind of dark magic—was easy to believe. It was much different than believing in Bill's elf magic. Magic shoes seemed friendly, maybe even helpful, despite Bill thinking Isabelle could have danced off her terrace. I hated to think what Tilly's magic could to my relationship. I felt sure it would be worse than a rumor.

I wanted to storm out of the room. After all the evil things she'd said to me since she'd arrived at the Village, thinking that I would come to her for help with anything was crazy.

But I had to stay calm. Not only because I was afraid of her, but also because there were visitors and residents watching to see what would happen next. If I wanted to squash this rumor about me and Chase, smiling and thanking her was the way to do it.

I briefly inclined my head. My neck felt so stiff with anger, I worried it might snap. "I certainly appreciate your offer of assistance. I hope you pass a pleasant day."

Every muscle in my body felt so rigid that I could barely force my legs out the door. How dare she ask such a thing? Like I would trust her with anything that might be close to me and Chase. There was no telling what kind of curse she'd put on us.

Tilly and Leo left immediately. I was so relieved to see them go. I sat at Bill's table as dozens of visitors came through the museum door. I hadn't been prepared for that discussion. My hands were still shaking.

Bill popped his head around the doorway just behind

some fake Siamese twins. I was so glad to see him. "You got out!"

"I have elf magic." He grinned and hugged me before he sat at his cutting table. "Looks like sales have been good so far."

"They'll be better with you here."

Chase followed Bill inside. He was so handsome in a plain gray suit, white shirt, and red tie.

I pulled him into the room where Tilly and I had just met and put my arms around him. "How did it go?"

"The DA refused to charge him. He said there were too many variables that didn't add up." He kissed me. "I think it was the elf magic that made everyone uncomfortable. They were afraid he might be crazy, just not crazy enough to have killed Isabelle."

"Elf magic is good for something after all."

"It got him out. But Detective Almond still thinks Bill is mocking the system by confessing and claiming it was magic shoes. He's not going to be far away from him until he can prove Bill is guilty, or find someone who is."

"I'm sorry. That's going to be hard for you." I touched his handsome face.

"For a while. I hope we can find the real killer quickly. You know we're gonna be swamped with reporters speculating on it until we do. I dislike reporters more than police."

"Who else do the police think could have killed Isabelle?" Manny joined us.

"I don't know. They're looking into the backgrounds of everyone in her retinue, and everyone working in the castle." Chase shrugged. "And keeping an eye on Bill. One wrong step and the DA could decide to change his mind about magic shoes."

I could see Chase was ready to get out of his suit and tie. "You should go home and change. I'm sure they need you at a hundred different places already."

"Yeah. I took texts all morning." He kissed me quickly

as a new flurry of visitors to the museum came in behind him. "Looks like the museum is enjoying good attendance. Adventureland will like that. That will make it easier to get your next show funded. I'll see you later."

The crowd kept us busy until noon. It slowed to a trickle then, as visitors headed to the various eateries for lunch. I knew they'd be back later when the heat of the day was growing. Everyone looked for cooler, inside fun after lunch.

"Lunch?" Manny suggested. "Even with Bill here, I suppose one of us should stay. I'll take the first shift."

"Thanks! I'm going to try to get to the bottom of all these rumors about me and Chase. There's something going on. I don't know what it is yet, but I'm going to figure it out. I bid you good day, sir. I shall see you in an hour."

"Good fortune to you, Lady Jessie!"

"Hey—will you bring me back a sandwich and a tankard of ale?" Bill requested. "I probably shouldn't leave again after being gone all morning."

"Sure."

I started down the cobblestones, not sure where I was going. Dozens of archers in brightly colored leather hailed me, their broad smiles interested, and muscles rippling. I was sure Robin Hood was checking them out. He was always looking for new Merry Men—and Women.

I thought Chase might have time for lunch. He had to eat, right? If I could catch him before he changed clothes and went back out, we could have lunch together.

I walked into the bottom floor of the Dungeon where the cries for help from jailed prisoners rent the air. They were just mannequins made up to look like pathetic people who'd been tortured and left to die. I scared two young boys who were wandering by the cells when I closed the outside door.

I have to admit that the crying and wailing isn't too bad during the day, but when Chase accidentally leaves the soundtrack on at night, it can be a little unnerving.

"Excuse me, good sirs." I made a curtsy to them and smiled to let them know it was still safe.

"Uh-hi." One of them smiled and spoke back.

"Have you seen the Bailiff? A big fellow with a braid wearing brown leather."

They glanced at each other. "No," the same child answered. "But we just got here."

"Thank you, my lads! A good day to you!" I checked upstairs anyway, carefully locking the door to the apartment after I went inside. I didn't want the kids following me. Chase had already changed and was gone. His gray suit and tie were on the bed.

With a sigh, I put them in the closet. At least he'd put his shirt in the hamper.

The boys downstairs were gone when I left the apartment. An older girl and boy had replaced them. They were flirting. He was trying to scare her. She was pretending that he was. Harmless fun.

I ignored them and went outside.

I glanced toward the Field of Honor. It was between jousting times so the large dirt field was empty. There were bleachers on either side where fans would cheer on their favorite knights. At the back of the field was the grandstand set up for royal personages and their guests. There was a joust in honor of the king and one in honor of the queen each day, as well as the Peasant's Joust.

I knew Chase was interviewing potential knights and scouting for jousters. Maybe he went to the field. We might still have time for a big pretzel with mustard and ale from the cart near the field.

There were many knights who lived in the Village, but only a select few were chosen to be in the jousts. The candidates had to be good with horses, have large egos, and be willing to do anything for the sake of applause.

To be fair, it wasn't easy working at the Field of Honor. I'd worked there for a few months as a squire one summer. It was amazing watching the riders as they went through their paces. They had to learn how to joust with another man coming at them with a large lance—making it appear real while not seriously injuring anyone.

But since the point was to knock your opponent from his horse, there were many strains, sprains, and backaches. None were life threatening because of the training.

Chase had worked at the field for a few years both as the Black Knight, and the Queen's Champion. Everyone had loved him and had been sorry to see him go when he decided to take on the role of the Village Bailiff.

I leaned against the heavy wood fence that surrounded the field. Even though there were no jousts at that time, a few interested residents and visitors were in the bleachers watching as the potential knights trained.

There were twelve men wearing lackey's clothes of colorful shirts and dark britches. They each wore a breastplate to protect their chests. Later they would be required to wear full armor if they made the cut.

I'd worn armor a few times for one reason or another. I'd never experienced anything hotter and more difficult to move in than a suit of metal. The ones used now were of lighter weight materials than they had been during the Middle Ages, but they were still like wearing a tin can with your arms and legs sticking out.

In the summer, that was like being in a soup can being cooked for lunch. Not a pleasant experience, yet hundreds of young men vied for their place to be jousters each hiring cycle. Not many lasted longer than a few months.

I'd been right. Chase was in the middle of everything. He'd left his leather at home, wearing his loose green shirt and brown britches with the breastplate that had been given to him by Queen Olivia. His dark hair was dusty and pulling free from his usual neat braid, but I could still hear girls sighing by the fence as they watched him demonstrate what would be required of a jousting knight.

He loved horses and had a large collection of miniatures he kept at the Dungeon. Horses seemed to love him too. They followed his slightest body movement and responded to what he needed them to do. It came easy for Chase. That's why he'd been so good at it.

"We'll be working with the lances today," he told the candidates. "Not against each other—not until you've mastered using them against the dummies. Everyone grab a lance and a horse and then line up, six in front of each target."

He hadn't noticed me yet. I thought about all the times I'd watched him working out here before we were together. He was always the star of the jousts, whether he was the evil Black Knight or receiving a rose from the queen as her champion. People in the bleachers had screamed his name.

"He should do the whole show by himself." A young woman wearing a knee-length blond wig and fairy wings was standing beside me. "I'd like to help him take off his armor every day."

She smiled at me with her glittery fairy face, a Pan's pipe hanging from her neck. Her dress, what little there was of it, was almost transparent in the sun.

I hated fairies. They might seem sweet and nice in stories, but here at the Village, they were devious and conniving. And they were always tiny and fragile-looking. None of them had size twelve shoes or were six feet tall.

"I don't think so." I smiled, wanting to run a lance into her. "You must be new here. He's married."

Her very blue eyes widened innocently. "I don't want to marry him. I'd just like to spend some time in one of the fountains with him—after he takes off his armor."

"Go away." I turned, too annoyed to play games with her. "I have magic dust in my pouch that kills fairies. I'd hate to see you dead on the cobblestones."

"Sorry. But this isn't a LARP. I'd just get up and run after him again. What is his wife thinking letting him out here alone like this?"

Since she wouldn't leave me alone, I moved away from that side of the fence. My friend, D'Amos Torres, worked with the animals in the Village. He was standing next to Hans Von Rupp, the Village blacksmith. They were watching the knights practice too.

"Jessie!" D'Amos smiled when he saw me. "Nice crop of new knights, huh? I really like the redhead in the blue breastplate. Who would've ever thought we'd see a female knight who wants to be a jouster?"

Chapter Six

It seemed I'd found the source of the rumor mill that was saying Chase and I were breaking up.

"Women don't belong out there," Hans said. "They'll only get hurt."

D'Amos laughed. "I've been watching this one for a few days. She has style and knows how to ride a horse."

Hans snorted. "She's still gonna get knocked out of her saddle a few times, and she'll come up crying. I don't think she belongs out there."

The horses and riders were lining up in front of the two dummies they would be attempting to hit with their lances. Safety always came first. Chase worked hard teaching the jousters not to have accidents.

I watched him lean over the rider in the blue breastplate—her hair was pinned up so it was hard to tell that she was a woman. He was adjusting something on her saddle. Or showing her a better way to hold the lance. People had injuries every year from holding the lance the wrong way.

Why didn't he tell me that he was training a female knight to joust?

Not that it mattered to me. I trusted Chase, but he had to know that his hands-on methods would become fodder for Village gossip. Just having a female knight would be enough to set idle tongues wagging. Since she was spending time with Chase that meant there was more to gossip about.

He probably didn't think anything of it. It was a job to him. He enjoyed training the knights. I was sure he didn't care if one of them was a woman.

But why didn't he tell me?

Hans had to go back to work at his shop. He was responsible for shoeing all the horses in the Village and sold specialty iron items he made at his forge.

D'Amos had once worked at the zoo in Columbia. We'd met years before when I was still teaching at the University there. I'd convinced him to come to the Village when he was ready to retire. Now he used his skills to keep a large group of animals—from elephants and camels to goats and pigs—healthy and happy. He also took care of the Cinderella carriages that visitors used for weddings and to tour the Village.

"I've heard the rumors," he said with no preliminary. "I hope you're not paying any attention to them. Chase loves you, Jessie. People are crazy if they think he cares about that Katharina woman. He's only training her like he is all those others."

"Katharina?"

"Yeah. She goes by one name, like Madonna or Liberace. She probably thinks people will pay more attention to her."

I wasn't sure if her name made any difference, but she had a good seat on her horse. She'd be notorious as the only woman rider. I wished I'd thought of it. I loved the Field of Honor. I thought there was some kind of rule about not having any women there. I didn't think to ask.

"You're not worried, are you?" D'Amos asked.

"No. Of course not. Chase has to wade through tons of fairies, princesses, and washing women every day. What makes Katharina so special?"

By this time, eleven of the twelve riders were on the ground. They'd either lost control of their horse or were pushed from the saddle when their lance hit its target. A few were laughing about it. Chase made a quick cut to get rid of eight of them who'd had the hardest time. Those riders left the field in disgrace but could still work as knights.

Three knights got up and grabbed their horses. Katharina was the only one to hit the target and stay on her horse. She was obvious to spot in the group as she removed her blue breastplate and shook loose her waist-length brown hair. Red highlights glinted in her tresses. I could hear the male sighs around me as they watched her.

"Oh yeah." D'Amos wiped his broad forehead with a cloth. "She's gonna be popular."

* * *

I waited at the side of the Field of Honor while the four knights remaining received a few further instructions from Chase before he let them go to the showers. The show was over. Watchers from the bleachers disappeared, most back to their jobs. A few knaves, squires, and vassals started working on preparing the field ready for the next joust. They had to smooth the dirt and put away the practice dummies. Everything had to be perfect for the King's Joust which was the last joust of the day.

Sir Marcus Bishop was coming toward me. He was a handsome young knight with his own Facebook page and a legion of fans that followed him everywhere. He always arrived early to sign autographs and prepare for the joust. He seemed to be in his early twenties. He had a big ego that matched his great skill with the horses—and the ladies—of the Village.

I decided that he would be a perfect match for Katharina. All I had to do was set them up. That would solve the

problem for me with the gossips, and the two of them could
be the stars of the show together. Everyone would love it.

"Lady Jessie." Marcus bowed deeply, but kept his
smiling blue gaze on mine. "You do me honor by attending
my joust."

"Save it for the women who don't already hate you," I
said. "I'm waiting for Chase."

"Of course you are."

"Have you seen the new jousting candidate?" Katharina
was already off the field, but I thought I could throw out my
first salvo toward their relationship. "She's a beauty and
good with a horse. Perfect for you."

"Women don't belong on the Field of Honor," he said in
a pleasant tone. "Women are perfect to help a man recover
from his arduous endeavors at the end of the day. They
shouldn't be knights."

So much for that campaign.

It was doubtful that Katharina would give her favor to a
knight who didn't support her attempt to become a jouster. I
wouldn't.

"Good day, Lady Jessie." Marcus smiled and saluted. He
hefted his duffle bag and started toward the stables.

Chase and Katharina were walking toward me, heads
bent close together, talking and laughing. My heart did a little
pitter-patter of jealousy before I could rein it back. D'Amos
was right. It was stupid for me to take stock in the gossip.

Katharina punched Sir Marcus in the arm as she passed
him. Clearly, it was intentional. Maybe there was hope for
them after all.

Marcus ignored her and continued to the stable behind
the royal grandstand.

Chase saw me and waved. "Jessie! There's someone I
want you to meet."

Katharina descended on me in all her glory. She was a
tall, muscular woman with an athletic body. She had
beautiful blue eyes, and smooth, tan skin. She was probably
somewhere in her twenties.

"Lady Jessie, this is Katharina, first female knight of Renaissance Village, and possibly the first woman jouster." Chase smiled at her as he spoke.

"Lady Jessie." Katharina curtsied. "I am honored to meet you. If it were not for the tutoring the Bailiff has given me, I am sure I would have fallen by the wayside."

"I'm sure you're being modest," I told her. "I was watching. You were good on the field today."

"Thank you very much. This is a lifelong dream for me. My father is Sir Reginald, one of the first knights to ever tread this hallowed soil. I have always wanted to be like him."

That surprised me. I didn't know that Sir Reginald had a family. He was always at the castle, and it was common knowledge that he'd had an affair with Queen Olivia. But that was years ago. Now he stayed on as one of the envoys of the royal couple. He'd had a formidable reputation at the Field of Honor when he was in his prime. He hadn't even put on a suit of armor in a long time.

"I know Sir Reginald," I returned. "I'm certain that he's happy to have you here."

"You'd think so." She pushed her hair out of her face with an impatient hand. The wind meshed the loose strands of her red-brown hair with Chase's dark strands.

I longed to tear them apart. Careful. Everyone is watching. They're waiting for you to act like you're jealous. Don't turn a few days of explanations into weeks of torment.

"So he's not a fan." I gritted my teeth as I said it. I just wanted to grab Chase and get him away from her.

"Alas, no." She smiled. "But I hope to win him over." She put a slender, gloved hand on Chase's shoulder. "We start private tutoring on the morrow. With the Bailiff's personal attention, I hope to be the best jouster ever."

That was all the polite Ren speech I could handle. She had not only let her hair come into contact with his, she touched him. And what was up with that not so subtle emphasis on personal?

"I'm sorry. We have to go. Good afternoon to you, Katharina." I suddenly realized that I'd been gone from the museum for a lot longer than an hour. Manny and Bill were probably starving.

"Where are we going?" Chase asked.

"Away from here," I growled.

It wasn't that Katharina had actually done anything wrong. She was beautiful, young, and strong. She was going to be a knight and a jouster. Chase was going to train her.

Why wasn't it me?

"Is something wrong, Jessie?" he asked in the dumbest voice ever.

"Why didn't you tell me that you were personally training a woman to be a jouster?" My long legs moved rapidly over the cobblestones. Maybe Bill was right and the sandals were magical. I was walking faster than Chase for once.

"What difference does it make? I tutor most of the new jousters. I thought you'd be thrilled that there's a woman candidate for jousting."

I stopped walking so abruptly that he almost ran into me. "What difference does it make? Every person I met in the Village today, including Tilly Morgenstern, told me how sorry they are that we're breaking up. Even Wanda knew about it. I thought they were all crazy—until I saw the two of you together."

He laughed.

Bad mistake.

"You can't be serious! After all this time, you think I'm interested in someone else? I can't believe you'd think I'd have anything to do with Katharina besides training," Chase complained. "I can't believe you don't trust me after we've been married almost a year."

Chase started walking quickly as his voice got louder.

"It's not that I don't trust you." I caught up with him. "But you can be blind to women throwing themselves at you. I've seen you ignore them many times."

"That's right." His dark eyes were angry. "I ignore them. Not that I think Katharina is throwing herself at me. Men look at you too, Jessie. I don't think you're involved with them. I know you and I are together. That's all that matters to me."

"Chase, everyone else is seeing this."

"Village gossip. You know that."

"And I didn't know there could be female jousters."

"There's no rule against it. Katharina wants to do it, and she's good on a horse. She's the best out of the pack you saw today. I don't see why she shouldn't be able to compete on the Field of Honor."

"But not with your personal attention," I argued. "If she's good, she'll make it. She doesn't need your help."

He stopped and stared at me right after we passed the Dutchman's Stage. "I'm not going to stop training her because you're jealous. That's crazy.

Out of the corner of my eye, I saw Tilly and Leo watching and listening. She giggled in her sweet little girl voice and went back inside Peter's Pub. Leo quickly followed.

Great. More gossip to add fuel to the fire.

"I'm not jealous," I quickly denied.

"Then what's the fuss about Katharina? I always train the new jousters and work with the knights."

I stopped walking again when we were close to Harriet's Hat House. "I don't think you're sleeping with Katharina, if that's what you're asking. I wonder why you didn't mention that she was a woman. You had to know the Village gossips would be running overtime."

He frowned. "You're right, Jessie. I didn't think about it that way. It was just another training session to me. I'm sorry."

He put his arms around me, and we kissed right out in the open. I heard a whooping sound and a voice called out. "I knew there was nothing really wrong with you two," Andre Hariot said. "Looks like I put my money in the right place."

I'd worked as Andre's apprentice at his hat shop one summer. He was a famous Hollywood hat maker and a romantic. Of course he'd be on my side.

Chase laughed. "See? Not everyone in the Village thought I was cheating on you. Andre was smart enough to know the truth."

"And bet on it, apparently." But I was smiling too. "I'm sorry too, Chase. I shouldn't have listened to the gossip."

He held my hand. "You wanted to be the first woman jouster?"

"Maybe." I pushed my short hair out of my face as the strong ocean breeze caught it. "A long time ago. Not now. I'm probably more jealous of that than anything."

"Thanks!" He grinned.

"You know what I mean."

Chase's radio went off—bad timing. Detective Almond was in the Village and wanted to see him at the castle. It seemed he'd found some other evidence in Isabelle's death.

Chapter Seven

I really wanted to hear what Detective Almond had to say, but I knew Bill and Manny had already waited a long time for lunch. I convinced Chase to give me a few extra minutes to grab two pretzels and ales for them. I dropped the ale and pretzels off at the museum—to a chorus of unappreciative groans—and we left right away.

The castle was still closed to visitors, even though the police had allowed the rest of the Village to open. There were dozens of police officers swarming over the castle like invaders. Were they looking for evidence that would link Bill to Isabelle's death, or trying to find other possible suspects?

Detective Almond, with his wrinkled shirt and too-tight pants, was on the sunny terrace overlooking the garden. Officers stood back for Chase and me to enter Isabelle's suite. "There you are, Manhattan! I was beginning to think you'd finally given up on this place and run away screaming like the rest of us!"

"Not yet," Chase said. "What's up?"

Detective Almond moved to the edge of the terrace near the wrought iron rail and looked down. "The medical examiner found a bit of torn fabric in Miss Franklin's hand. We think she snatched it from her attacker as she was being tossed over the edge."

He held up a plastic bag that contained a small fragment of green material. It looked as though it could have come from a shirt, not unlike the one Chase was wearing. It was standard issue from Stylish Frocks, the shop that created all of the costumes for the Village. They outfitted residents and visitors alike, as well as selling their costumes.

Chase glanced at me as he took the bag from Detective Almond and held it up in the sunlight. "This could belong to anyone."

"But it probably came from a man's shirt, right?" He nodded toward Chase's green shirt.

"No," I added. "Women wear them too. There are probably a hundred people here today wearing shirts like that."

"Well, I might have to check them all," Detective Almond said. "Or I might find that shirt in Bill Warren's closet. What do you think?"

"I can take you there, and we can check," Chase volunteered. "If you have a search warrant."

"Search warrant, huh?" Detective Almond's perpetual frown deepened. "Since when do I need a warrant to search the Village?"

Chase shrugged. "Since Adventureland said so. It's not my rule. You can talk to the king and queen about it."

"It's getting to the point that it might be easier to close this whole place down." Detective Almond stared down into the houses and shops beyond Mirror Lake and ending at the Field of Honor."

"I don't think it would be as easy as all that," Chase disagreed. "But you do what you have to do. I follow the regs and work as liaison between you and the Village. I do what I have to do."

The tension was much thicker between the two of them than was normal. Usually they worked well together. Was it only because I'd made Chase wait for me? Or was something else up between them that I didn't know about?

Detective Almond got on his cell phone and called for a warrant. "It will take about an hour. I'd like you and Jessie to stay here at the castle until it gets here. I want to be the first one to check Bill Warren's clothing, if you don't mind. I know you want the shoemaker to be innocent of all this. What I don't know is how far you'd go to accomplish it."

"I wouldn't do anything to impede your investigation," Chase said. "Having this hang over the Village isn't good for us either."

"I figure Warren was the last person to see Isabelle Franklin alive. Someone picked her up and dumped her into the garden. She was wearing the slippers he admitted to giving her. I'd say there is something going on besides magic shoes."

"Just being in the castle doesn't make him a killer." I defended Bill.

"And you know Bill Warren well, do you Jessie? Because he told me he's only known the two of you for a few weeks. Good thing he has that elf magic, huh? That takes care of everything."

"You can clearly tell by him wanting to take responsibility for Isabelle's death—however misplaced—that he didn't kill her." I was starting to get hot. "A real killer wouldn't have made up a story about magic if he was accused."

"Unless he wanted all of us to think he was crazy." Detective Almond smiled. "We don't like the insanity plea here in South Carolina. I just want you to know that. I'm going to get enough real evidence that I don't need anyone to confess."

Detective Almond stepped to the far end of the terrace, cell phone in hand, as he answered a call. "I think one of my officers may have found something," he said before hurrying downstairs.

Chase and I stayed on the terrace. We watched Detective Almond collect something from an officer. He put it in another plastic bag and glanced up at us with a smile.

"That can't be good," I remarked. "He looks too happy."

"I hope we're not wrong about Bill," Chase said. "Detective Almond says he has a gut feeling about him. I don't like going against him when we're supposed to be working together."

"Is that what's wrong between you?"

"No. He offered me a job again when I was at the station with Bill. He was really serious about it—even made a mock-up of a badge with my name on it."

I rolled my eyes toward the blue skies above us. "How many times is he going to ask you when you've already said no a dozen times?"

Chase looked deeply into my eyes. "He said the police are going to demand a bigger police presence at the Village in the next fiscal year. He also said that presence would have to be monitored by a real member of the police department. It can't be me unless I join up."

I hugged him. "That's not what you want to do, right? You could've been a police officer anytime."

"Maybe this is different."

"No it's not. You can give up the job. You can learn a skill or something, and we'll move out of the Dungeon into a shop with an apartment. It would be great. We've talked about it before."

"But never seriously."

I didn't know what else to say. He sounded unhappy with the idea of not being Bailiff. I thought it might be a good thing—no calls late at night—or during important conversations. As long as I picked good exhibits for the museum, I was set. Chase could learn to do something else. Maybe carve wood horses.

He finally smiled and kissed me. "I'm not really worried about it, Jessie. They've talked about it before. We'll see what happens."

"Right."

We found chairs on the terrace. It was hot up there. On the ground below, police officers were scurrying around like insects.

"I really don't think Bill did this," I finally said, feeling the need to say something. "You didn't see him with Isabelle yesterday. They were like cream and sugar together. I know he didn't know her well, and she might have rejected him after he brought her the slippers. But you remember how patient and slow moving he was making the boots when we met him in Tennessee. He doesn't strike me as someone with a sudden outburst of temper that could kill someone."

Chase shook his head, his eyes still on what was happening in the garden. "I agree with you about Bill taking responsibility for his elf magic. He really believes he has magic. I talked to him while we were waiting for his last interview at the police station. He even thinks the police not being able to charge him is proof of his magic. When he confessed to killing Isabelle, he was serious. He thinks his dancing slippers ran away with her."

"Which might be why Detective Almond thinks he's pretending to be crazy."

He grinned and reached for my hand. "We're all crazy, or we wouldn't be here."

"That's the truth." I linked my fingers with his.

"I'm sorry if training Katharina embarrassed you, Jessie. But this is Renaissance Village. It's always going to be something. I didn't think about the impact it might have on you. I'll stop working with her, if you want me to."

"You don't have to stop training her. I wish I could have been a knight. Can you imagine me as a jouster? I would've been awesome."

He squeezed my hand. "You're already awesome. But there's no reason you can't joust if you want to go through the training. I'll help you."

"No. I'm too busy at the museum to train to be a knight."

I smiled at him. "Just a heads-up would be nice next time if you're involved personally with any beautiful women. That way I'm prepared for it."

"Fair enough, but I expect the same courtesy."

"Sure. But I never get to work with gorgeous, sexy men. Maybe I should look for a sexy craftsman next time."

"As long as you come home to me every night." He kissed my fingers.

"So what are we going to do about this thing with Bill? Have you told Detective Almond about the passageways in the castle? Anyone could have gotten in and out after killing Isabelle."

"I'm meeting with King Harold later today to discuss that. He doesn't want the police searching the passages. I think he'll have to deal with it, but I want him to know it's going to happen."

"There's something else too, Chase. Yesterday at the museum, Isabelle took down Sir Dwayne a peg or two. I've been wondering if he stewed about it long enough and finally flipped out when he saw her with Bill."

"That sounds possible, and another angle for Detective Almond to check. Although I've never seen Dwayne in anything as ordinary as green cotton. He's more the silk and satin type."

"Maybe he figured everyone knew him that way and changed it up. He might have even dressed differently to try to frame Bill for Isabelle's death."

"Possible." He pointed to the suddenly empty garden. "Let's see what else he found."

It only took Detective Almond a few minutes to come back upstairs. He was still carrying the plastic bag we'd seen him use to collect evidence. "Looks like we've got something else."

Chase took a look at the bag. "I think it's a leather string. Maybe a shoelace."

"Something a shoemaker might have, right?" Detective Almond rocked back on his heels. "I've got my search warrant, Sir Bailiff. Lead the way to the shoemaker's house."

I followed them out of Isabelle's suite and through the castle, but as we reached the front gate, Rita Martinez gestured to me. I excused myself, saying I wanted to pay my respects to the king and queen. Chase smiled and said he'd see me later. Detective Almond kind of grunted and kept walking.

Rita was waiting in one of the downstairs alcoves. It was an area off-limits to visitors, where the king and queen's private chambers began. There were dozens of rooms in the castle for VIPs as well. With a full staff to look after them, and the best of everything, Adventureland employees were frequently rewarded with a stay here.

"Jessie, I saw something yesterday while I was in the garden." Rita's dark eyes flitted up and down the empty corridor as though she was watching for someone. "It was too long before Isabelle died, but I'm not sure if I shouldn't mention it."

"Did you tell the police?"

"No. I wasn't going to tell anyone, but Bill is such a nice man. I hate the idea that he'd go to prison for something he didn't do."

I knew many residents in the Village had secret pasts. Rita could be one of them. She'd been a fixture at the castle for years, probably since it was built from the old Air Force communication tower. She ruled over the kitchen with a firm hand, as I'd found out when I first came to work there.

"What did you see?"

"It was one of Isabelle's ladies arguing with her on the terrace." Rita checked the corridor again. "I couldn't hear what they were saying. Isabelle liked to belittle people who worked for her. I don't know why anyone chose to be part of her retinue."

"I never understood either," I agreed. "But she didn't deserve to be killed."

"There were days . . ."

"I know. You'll have to tell the police, Rita. They won't

want to hear it secondhand."

"I can't. I'm not exactly who you think I am." She smiled, but her lips trembled. "Before I came here, I went through a rough patch. I can't tell them who I am, or it would take over my life here too."

I was exceedingly curious. I wanted to ask more about her secret life. But I could see she was upset, so I tabled the discussion. "Let me think about it. Maybe there's some way for me to say it. I want to tell the police about Isabelle shaming Sir Dwayne at the museum too. I can tell Detective Almond about that, and maybe mention her relationship with her ladies."

"The ladies, definitely," Rita drawled. "Sir Dwayne has always been good to her. I've never heard him say a cross word to anyone."

That didn't fit my image of Sir Dwayne who had struck me as being a bully at the museum. I was sure Rita had her own reasons to defend him.

Rita hugged me. "Thank you, Jessie. Please try to keep my name out of it."

"Just one thing—why were you smoking in the garden? I thought everyone smoked in the courtyard."

"Just for a change. I don't know. Sometimes I sneak out there to enjoy the greenery."

She thanked me again and scurried away.

I sighed when I thought about finding Detective Almond. Manny needed a real break. I convinced myself I should take care of that first and then tell the police what I'd heard and seen.

The Village was filled to capacity despite the hot summer day. Of the thousands of visitors, a large group was wearing the red nametags that identified them as possible replacements for the Village. Jugglers, bubble blowers, men and women dressed as cows and horses, passed me. There were several unicorns with flowered harnesses and painted hooves. I really liked a singing troubadour wearing red satin. He had a wonderful voice and was nice to look at too. I marked him down in my book.

There was still a line waiting to get into the museum. That was exciting since the refreshments and music were long gone. It looked as though my shoemaker was going to draw the largest crowd ever.

"Thank goodness you got back," Manny said after I had fought my way up the stairs. "I'm parched, and that pretzel only left me hungry. What happened at the castle?"

I gave him the fifty-cent tour, which brought him up to speed. As we spoke, I watched Bill with the visitors. They were spellbound by him. His hands moved slowly across the leather as he worked. He kept up a dialog about his elf ancestors that seemed to captivate his audience.

I sent Manny off for an hour. I'd have Bill take a break when the museum wasn't so busy.

A pretty, young woman wearing a green snood lifted her skirt so Bill could look at her foot. As with Isabelle, he went into raptures over the beauty of her instep and her toes.

"Please sit here and I'll fit these boots on you, my dear." Bill got up from his chair and took the woman's hand. She giggled as she sat in his spot, crossed one leg over the other, and held up her foot.

Gallantly, Bill got down on one knee with a boot in his hand. Cameras clicked and flashes illuminated the museum as visitors took plenty of pictures. I wished I could take a picture too, but the Royal Photographer was gone already, and residents weren't allowed to have such devices. I could only hope Bill had put on a good show while the photographer was still there.

He tickled the girl's foot. "What do you want to do in these boots?"

She smiled and hid behind a pretty green fan. "I'd like to walk quickly and comfortably everywhere I go."

Bill lowered his head as though he were whispering to the boots while he laced them on her narrow feet. "There you are. Try them out—but beware. Others have been taken over by the magic I put into them. I wouldn't want that to happen to you."

The young woman in green and gold got to her feet with his help. Suddenly, one of her feet started jumping around as though she'd lost control of it. "Oh! What's happening?"

"You'd better sit down," Bill said. "That may have been too much magic."

But before she could do as he said, she began jumping and running around the museum. She cried out that her feet were running away with her. She didn't appear able to stop. People moved out of her way as she leapt between them, kicking and sprinting like an athlete.

"Please, please help me stop. I'm scared. Take the magic back."

The curious crowd moved in even closer when they heard her cry out. The bulk of the crowd separated Bill from the woman. I tried to reach her, not sure what was going on. I couldn't get through the visitors packed tightly around me, watching in awe.

"Hold on!" Bill yelled. "I'll help you."

The woman kept hopping, skipping toward the front door. There was no way to close it with so many people in the way. She was jumping down the stairs toward the cobblestones when I ran after her. I grabbed the end of her gown and tackled her. We rolled from the bottom stairs toward the green grass that separated the Art and Craft Museum from the Antique Weapons Museum next door.

"Thank you. Thank you." She hugged me to her.

"That's okay. Let's get these boots off your feet." I noticed that her feet were still moving even though she wasn't walking anymore. It was crazy—and maybe elf magic.

Was this what Bill was suggesting had happened to Isabelle?

Chapter Eight

The event swelled the crowds of visitors even more as word spread quickly around the Village.

I was completely amazed that the green and gold lady bought the boots she'd been wearing as well as two more pairs. A rush on Bill's boots soon found his entire stock sold out. He stayed on at the museum working, even though his stall had to be shut down.

Despite the numbers of people who wanted to see the shoemaker with elf magic, I still shut the exhibit for an hour to give Bill a break. He looked pale, and his hands were trembling. I knew he needed some time to recuperate.

Merlin had some words for me when he learned that I'd shut the museum. He found me, Manny, and Bill sitting at an outdoor table near the Good Luck fountain.

"You don't just walk away from a feature attraction." Merlin paced through the grass. "We're getting calls. People want to see the shoemaker."

I finished chewing my pretzel and shot back, "We all

needed a break. We'll open again soon."

"Not soon enough," the wizard ranted. "Bad management sinks ships. Keep that in mind, young woman. Get that museum open again."

He stalked away, his starred robe flying out around him. I heard one older lady cry out as he passed her.

"The man can't help but flash what he has." I smiled at Manny.

My assistant didn't return my smile. "Merlin sounded serious, Lady Jessie. Perhaps we should return to the museum."

"We'll go back when Bill is ready."

Bill didn't look ready for witty banter with visitors just yet. He'd eaten a little of his turkey leg and sipped some ale. "I'm going to run to the privies first, if you don't mind. That elf magic can take a lot out of you."

We waited until Bill had disappeared behind the Romeo and Juliet stage.

"I wish you'd been there when that woman started running around like a crazy person," I said to Manny. "Even after I'd tackled her, her legs kept moving. I don't know what to think."

Manny grinned. "Elf magic?"

"I guess so. It didn't seem normal to me. And look what it did to my shoemaker."

"He seems upset by it. Perhaps using elf magic is hard on a person."

Chase joined us in time to hear Manny's remark. "I've heard about the magic boots. It's all over the Village. What happened?"

I went through the basic event for him. "Unless that woman was some kind of plant from Adventureland, she was really affected by the boots. Bill didn't look surprised, only concerned. Maybe he really did put the slippers on Isabelle and she hopped right off the terrace."

"Maybe." Chase took a piece of my pretzel as he sat in the grass. "One thing I can tell you is that none of Bill's clothes or boots matched the green material or the strip of leather Detective Almond found in the garden. It doesn't clear Bill, but it didn't add any ammunition against him. Right now, all the police have is Bill's confession to putting too much magic into Isabelle's slippers, and that he was at the castle."

"Being at the castle hardly seems significant," Manny returned. "There are hundreds of people at the castle every day."

"He's right." I gave Chase the rest of my pretzel and ale. It was probably all he'd had to eat and drink. "What about the hidden passages in the castle? Is the king going to let you brief Detective Almond?"

"He already sent word that I should take the police through the passages." Chase shrugged. "I can't say finding out there was a secret way in and out of Isabelle's suite made Detective Almond happy. That meant there could be hundreds of suspects that weren't seen by Isabelle's retinue. He stopped for lunch at Bawdy Betty's. I think he couldn't tackle the idea on an empty stomach."

"But what if Bill really has elf magic and accidentally caused Princess Isabelle to fall?" Manny asked. "We must consider that possibility as well."

Chase shook his head. "I'm not considering elf magic as the means of her death unless there's nothing else possible. I know the police won't buy it."

"Why is that? People have seen remarkable things happen here. When I told my parents about your wedding, they summoned a witch to make sure I wasn't cursed." Manny nodded behind me as he finished speaking. "Bill is returning."

"Hi Chase," Bill said. "I'm feeling better now, Jessie. Maybe we should head back to the museum before Merlin has a hissy fit."

Chase got to his feet. "I need you to tell me the truth. Did you hire that woman today to sell more boots? No one would blame you. Does it tie into what happened to

Isabelle?"

Bill laid a hand on his heart. "As God is my witness, I
didn't hire that woman. I think my elf magic may be affected
by magic in the Village, making it stronger. I can feel it all
around me. It might be out of control."

"Why didn't you mention your magic when we first
met?" I asked.

"You learn to keep your mouth closed about such
things." He scuffed one of his beautiful boots in the grass.
"Back home, people don't believe in magic. I didn't mention
it until we got here and I realized that this was the right place
for me—in more than one way. I'm sorry about Isabelle—
and that woman at the museum today. I'll go lighter on the
magic."

"About Isabelle," Chase said. "Did you actually see her
dance off the terrace?"

"No. She didn't want me to put the slippers on her. I left
them with her. It didn't work out the way I'd planned. You
were right about her, Jessie. Even my elf magic wasn't
enough."

Chase didn't mention the items they'd looked for in
Bill's room. He had to leave quickly to work with the new
knights and jousters between events at the Field of Honor. He
kissed me and whispered in my ear. "We're good with this,
right?"

"We're good." I smiled. "Go do your job."

Manny was grinning as Chase left. "I'm so glad you two
aren't breaking up."

"You and Chase are breaking up?" Bill asked.

I rolled my eyes. "Let's get back to the museum.
Everything else will be fine."

We followed the cobblestones to Squire's Lane. The
three, large red brick houses near the Main Gate had sat
empty for years before I'd proposed putting the Art and Craft
Museum into one of them. The Antique Weapons Museum
had come next. I hadn't heard what was going into the third
house. Maybe it would be a museum about magic since that

seemed to be so popular.

Hundreds of residents, including Hephaestus who owned the Peasant's Pub on the other side of the King's Highway, passed us. I also said hello to Lady Cathy from the crochet shop. A large group of pirates was swaggering through the area for show, as they did several times a day. Rafe, the pirate king, was at the lead. His long black hair, gold teeth, and massive mustache made him quite a sight for the visitors.

There were so many people trying out for parts. A woman who looked like a pink poodle waved and smiled at me. Her hair was piled so high on her head that it reminded me of the woman Chase had been talking about yesterday.

Another man was clearly imitating Harry Houdini. He wore a plastic box filled with water over most of his body. I wouldn't recommend him for a permanent role. Manny shuddered when he saw him.

Two people were dressed like large, sparkly fish. I thought they might do well at the Mermaid Lagoon near the entrance.

"Do any of these actors actually end up working here?" Manny asked.

"Sure. It's how we fill the ranks after the end of summer turn over. They might not all keep their costumes. A few of them will be hired to replace characters we already had."

We'd reached the museum. There was still a long line of visitors waiting to get inside.

"I guess we'll be busy this afternoon," Bill muttered as we started up the stairs.

"Just go a little lighter on the magic, huh?" I asked him. "That woman could've fallen down the stairs and been seriously injured today."

Maybe he had elf magic. Maybe he didn't. Whatever worked for him was good for the museum and the Village as long as no one got hurt.

"You don't have to tell me!" Bill took his place at the table where he worked. He had orders he was already filling. He smoothed out a large piece of supple tan leather and then put the pattern that he used to cut a boot to size on top of the leather. People moved closer as he began cutting.

Everyone was talking about the excitement of that morning. I was surprised at how many visitors wanted their boots to run away with them. Maybe that was part of the magic.

Manny and I stood near the door making sure that people who were leaving went out on the right side so there was room for people to come in on the left side. The afternoon was too hot for the ceiling fans to make much difference. I could feel the hot, humid air pushing at me even though I was used to it.

I saw Detective Almond approaching before he saw me. I was worried that he'd come to take Bill away again for more questioning. I was ready to offer excuses as to why he should wait.

But he wasn't there for Bill. He wiped his brow and panted as he reached the top of the stairs. "I know you worked in the castle for a while, Jessie. You must know about the secret passages. How about taking me on the grand tour?"

Chapter Nine

"Me? Why me?"

"Because my Bailiff seems to want to help my suspect."

"I do too. I'd be just as likely to lead you down the wrong passage—maybe more likely." I couldn't believe he wanted me to take him through the castle.

His eyes narrowed. "Yeah. But you're not prepared, are you? Let's go."

What could I say? I told Manny I was leaving for a while. Detective Almond and I walked out of the museum accompanied by two uniformed officers.

"So what about this elf magic thing?" he asked as we started toward the castle.

I knew then why he'd wanted me to show him the passages. He wanted to talk to me about Bill, probably hoping I'd say something to give him away that Chase hadn't said. As I'd observed before, Detective Almond seemed slow and wasn't exactly a snappy dresser, but he was sneaky when it came to solving his cases.

"I'm not sure. Bill didn't mention his magic when we

met him in Tennessee. Once we got here, everything was
fine, until yesterday when Isabelle came for a pair of slippers.
That's when he first told me about the magic."

We were passing the Mermaid Lagoon as the pirate ship
Queen's Revenge was sailing across Mirror Lake. Her
billowing white sails were beautiful against the clear blue
sky. I could hear the pirates shouting at each other across the
water.

Detective Almond was only interested in the scantily
clad mermaids who waved and blew kisses to him. "Hi there.
You ladies have it made on a day like this, don't you? The
water is the place to be. And taking a few clothes off is a
good idea."

The girls flapped their shiny tails at him, and one of
them started singing a suggestive song as she combed her
long blond hair. It was only a wig and a fake tail, but it really
attracted the male part of our visitor population in the
summer.

He chuckled as he finally tore himself away from the
mermaids. "What were you saying, Jessie?"

"Maybe I should put on a bikini top and a tail so you can
hear me."

"So I'm having a little fun in an otherwise boring place.
Shoot me."

"Boring?" We were far enough up the hill toward the
castle to look down on the beautiful Village. "I don't know
how you can say that. This place is more full of life than
anywhere I've ever been. You must be jaded from working
here when the Village first opened."

The tall policeman on my right snickered. "You used to
work here, Detective? I thought you hated this place."

"Mind your own business, Barkley," Detective Almond
snapped back. He lowered his tone as he grabbed my arm.
"I'd rather not tell everyone that I was the first Bailiff here, if
you don't mind. I'd lose some respect with the way everyone
feels about it."

"Well, don't call it boring again." I had to slow down as

he continued walking with my hand through his arm. His tiny little legs couldn't keep up with my long ones.

"Okay. I get it. You love it here. But you gotta admit the place is a pain in the butt. Too many people and not enough cops. Before you say it, Chase does a great job with what he's got. He just doesn't have enough manpower. I've suggested to the chief many times that we put uniforms out here. I suppose Chase told you about the job offer."

"He did."

"Well?"

I didn't want to talk to him about what Chase might or might not do. So I changed the subject. "Why haven't they put officers here?"

He shrugged. "The chief says we lose too many officers that way. You know what's happened to the officers we've put here in the past. I think I have a plan to stop that."

I laughed. "I know one of them is sailing by us right now as a pirate."

"Enough of that." He waved his hand. "What do you think Bill is doing to make those boots of his magic? Drugs? Hypnotism?"

I was glad he didn't bring up the idea of Chase working directly for the police again. "I don't know. Nothing was said about magic boots until that woman this morning. Now it's all anyone can talk about. Maybe you should question her. Bill claims he didn't hire her to act that way. But maybe he did. It sure helped boot sales."

"I'll do that." He took out a small, mangled notebook. "What was her name?"

"I don't know. I tackled her and pulled the boots off. I didn't ask who she was. She bought boots afterward. Maybe you can find her receipt."

"Funny, Jessie. How many people are here today? How many of them are buying magic boots?"

"Thousands, I hope. You know Adventureland likes a good profit."

We had reached the entrance to the castle, passed The

Feathered Shaft where archers were practicing shooting at targets made of hay. To the right, across the cobblestones, was Merlin's Apothecary, the Merry Mynstrel's Stage, and the first aid station where Wanda had once worked.

I saw Wanda's ghost watching visitors with sprained ankles, skinned knees, and just plain overheated as they went in and out of the station. There was a tent beside it where visitors and residents could walk through a light shower to cool down. The problem was that many of the costumes were expensive and could be hurt by water. That left a large group gulping water and dipping their hands into the fountains around the Village to cool off.

Wanda shot toward us like a speeding blue bullet as soon as she saw me walking up the hill with the police. Great. Not only would I have to walk Detective Almond through the secret passages in the castle, I'd have to do so as I ignored her stupid banter.

Two, well-built men who seemed to be dressed like Hercules—wearing only animal skin loin cloths— came out of the cool-down tent, dripping with water, and laughing. Wanda took one look at them and abandoned her quest to follow me.

Thank goodness for partially dressed young men with healthy bodies!

"Let's walk a little faster," I urged Detective Almond. "The castle has air conditioning. I don't know about you, but I'm roasting out here."

He couldn't walk as fast as I could, but he managed to put out a little burst of speed. He showed his badge to Gus at the gate, and we passed inside quickly.

I glanced at Gus, thinking again about him being gone from the gate when Isabelle was killed. Not that I thought he would have killed her either—but I was curious about his absence.

Immediately inside the castle was the Great Hall where the King's Feast is held every Sunday evening. There was no air conditioning here, but the heavy concrete walls made it cooler anyway.

"You ever been to one of these feasts?" Barkley asked Detective Almond.

"Too many. A lot of bragging and Cornish hens. Not much else to see."

"Not true at all." I defended the feast. "All of the shops are represented that night. There is jousting and daring horse tricks, swordplay, and chivalry. Not to mention ladies, lords, and jugglers. It's a great event. I'll be glad to give you free tickets for the next one."

Barkley nudged his partner, and they both nodded.

"Could we get back to why we're here?" Detective Almond demanded as the officers opened the heavy doors that separated visitors from the main part of the castle. "Where do these secret passages start, Jessie?"

"They were created to make all the rooms in the castle easy to reach for the staff. They get calls all during the day and night for food and things I don't want to think about. The passages start in the kitchen and spread through the whole place."

"Then let's start here." He stood back for me to precede him into the kitchen.

The castle kitchen was a large, restaurant-type kitchen with several stoves, dozens of workstations, and long lengths of countertop. There were huge pantries, refrigerators, freezers, and hundreds of cooking utensils hanging from the walls and ceiling. The cooks here made food for hundreds of people every Sunday night. There were dozens of workers running back and forth to do the bidding of the chefs.

Rita was at the center of everything as she coordinated the requests from the people who were staying at the castle along with the residents who lived there. She was a small, energetic woman who seemed to see everything. At least that's what I'd thought when I worked for her.

"Jessie." She stared at the three men with me. "What are you doing here?"

"I'm taking Detective Almond and his officers through

the passages." There was a beautiful ice cream sundae on the counter beside me. I wished I could dive right into it. "They're looking for information about Isabelle."

Her face became sharp. "I believe they'll need permission from King Harold to do that."

"Excuse me—we already have permission from the king." Detective Almond sounded impatient. "We're going through the passages. Please get out of the way."

Rita jumped in front of the entrance to the passages and spread her arms across the door. "I need to talk to King Harold before you go inside."

I wondered what was wrong with her. What could she be protecting in the passages? I'd been in there yesterday, and they'd looked like they always did.

Detective Almond signaled to his officers to get Rita out of the way.

Before they could get physical, I asked for a moment to speak to her alone. Maybe if I understood what she was doing, I could help.

"You've got two minutes." Detective Almond grudgingly gave us.

Rita and I went into one of the supply pantries and shut the door. She was still nervous and fidgety.

"He's going in there whether you want him to or not," I explained. "Did you kill Isabelle?"

Rita was small, but I knew from experience that she was strong. She could throw fifty-pound bags of flour and sugar into the pantry with no problem. She could probably have managed to throw Isabelle off the terrace.

"Of course not! Why would I kill her? She was mean and petty, but I didn't want to see her dead."

"Then what? What are you trying to hide?"

She started crying.

This was going to take way longer than two minutes.

"You asked why I was smoking in the garden. I was . . . meeting someone."

"Someone from the castle," I encouraged her to explain

quickly. "Who was it?"

"It was Sir Dwayne. I'm worried that he might be accused of killing Isabelle."

Suddenly I understood. "You and Sir Dwayne were—" I made hand gestures that brought a blush to her face. "Really?"

"Why do you say it like that, Jessie? So I'm not as young as I used to be. Does that mean I have to be alone the rest of my life?"

"No. Of course not." But Sir Dwayne?

"We met in the garden sometimes when he could get away from Isabelle's demands. You know how she could be."

"How does that relate to the passages?"

"He's been missing since Isabelle died." Rita twisted her work-roughened hands together. "I thought he might be hiding in the passages. I looked for him, but I couldn't find him."

There was a polite rap at the door. "Are you ladies almost finished in there?" Detective Almond asked.

"You have to tell him," I whispered. "He's gonna keep sniffing around until he finds out anyway. You're making yourself look guilty."

"I can't," she muttered. "Everyone will know, and they'll laugh at me behind my back."

I took her hands in mine and stared into her tortured eyes. "They already know, Rita. That's the way the Village is."

The pantry door opened slightly. "I'm going into the secret passages now," Detective Almond said. "Is there something I should know?"

I pushed the door open. "Rita has something to tell you. Maybe you could come in here for a minute."

"I'm not hiding in the pantry, Jessie. Whatever she has to say, she can say out here."

"Please," I whispered. "She's embarrassed to say it out there."

He wore a look of someone almost beyond their patience, but he came into the pantry and shut the door behind him. "This better be good."

After Rita had confessed her secret sins with Sir Dwayne, Detective Almond nodded. "So you haven't seen Sir Dwayne since Isabelle was killed? Are you sure? You're not hiding him somewhere?"

"No. If I were hiding him, why would I be worried about what you'd find in the passages?" She held her chin high. "I could hide him in a thousand different places that you'd never find."

"Okay. Let's go through the passages. If we find him there, I'll have to question him like I have everyone else." He looked her over. "You know this could make you a suspect in this case. Maybe you wanted Sir Dwayne all to yourself and decided to take out the competition."

Rita snorted. "I know many ways to kill someone with food that your medical examiner would never know. I wouldn't have pushed her off the terrace."

Detective Almond wrote her words in his notebook. "Good to know. I'm glad I don't normally eat at the castle."

She had made her point, though. He didn't ask her any other questions about Isabelle's death. He and I, and the two officers, went into the passage from the kitchen. Rita closed the door behind us.

Chapter Ten

Even though there were lights along the edges of the passage, it still took a moment to get used to the dimness. I noticed that the officers were nervous as we started out. They both held their guns, ready for trouble. I led the way with Detective Almond coming up behind me.

It was much cooler in the passages, a relief from the hot summer sun. I walked slowly knowing that they were looking for clues. Or Sir Dwayne. I hoped Isabelle's last boyfriend wasn't using this as a hiding place. The passage was too tight for a scuffle with armed police without someone getting hurt.

"Where are we going, Jessie?" Detective Almond asked as I passed an intersection.

"I thought you'd want to go right to Isabelle's suite. It's this way."

"And all these other passages?"

"They go to the other suites, chambers, and various places in the castle."

"When were these put in? I don't remember the castle

being like this when I worked here."

"I thought they were designed when it was built." I shrugged. "I guess if they weren't, then I don't know. Maybe Merlin, or the king and queen, could answer that."

We all heard a sound. The officers flattened their bodies against the cool concrete wall. Detective Almond put his hand over my mouth and gestured for quiet.

"What is that?" he whispered.

I removed his pudgy fingers from my lips. "It's probably a TV or something. It could be someone talking. You can hear everything from here. It all depends on where you're standing."

We listened a few more minutes until it was clear that someone on the other side of the wall was watching an episode of Star Trek.

Detective Almond nodded. "Let's move on."

We were almost to Isabelle's suite when I noticed something on the floor near the secret entrance. It wasn't big enough to be Sir Dwayne, but it hadn't been there the day before.

"What's that?" Barkley pointed.

"Shine a flashlight over here," Detective Almond told him.

The four of us looked as the bright beam of light picked up a piece of green material. I started to lift it, but Detective Almond held me back. "That could be where the piece of material came from that was in Isabelle's hand. We need to bag that before it gets contaminated."

Officer Barkley put on latex gloves and held up the material. "It's one of those Ren Faire shirts like they all wear, sir."

"Put it in the bag," Detective Almond said. "Is that blood on it?"

Barkley and his partner closely examined the shirt. "Hard to tell in this light. But it looks like it could be."

They were trying to stuff the large shirt into the small bag when we heard a scraping sound from the other side of the wall. The door from behind the bookshelf opened and light poured into the passage.

"I thought I was taking you through the passages," Chase said. "What happened?"

Detective Almond put together a few nonsensical reasons why he hadn't waited for Chase. I knew they weren't true, but I decided not to make a big deal out of it at that moment. I could always explain to Chase later.

I was glad I'd been there for Rita anyway. She might not have been willing to make the connection with Chase that she'd made with me. It was a woman thing.

"Anyway," Detective Almond concluded. "Now that you're here, Manhattan, you might as well go through the rest of the passages with us. Thank you for your help, Jessie. I hope you'll keep what happened here today under your hat. I know how the Village likes to gossip."

Chase raised his brows in a questioning manner as we exchanged places. I shrugged, hoping he understood that it wasn't a good time to talk about it.

I was glad for him to finish the rest of the tour with the police. They probably needed me at the museum.

I closed the door and then the bookcase hiding the entrance to the passage. There were still crime scene people and police officers working in Isabelle's suite. I got out quickly, not wanting to be involved in their investigation.

I made my way back down to the castle entrance, thinking about Rita, Isabelle, and Sir Dwayne. I could understand Rita trying to protect Sir Dwayne, but it was interesting that she thought he could be guilty. At least her confession to Detective Almond put a different spin on who the killer could be—a killer who wasn't Bill.

Maybe she was just doing what I'd done with Bill—give him a chance if the police started looking his way.

I was happy to share that information with Bill during a brief afternoon break. The museum was packed with visitors when I got back. It was my first opportunity to tell him the good news.

He didn't take it the way I'd expected him to. "I still feel responsible for that beautiful girl's death. I know you don't believe in my magic, Jessie, but it's real. And sometimes it can be harmful."

Manny and I exchanged glances. He didn't remark on the subject, just sipped his green tea that we'd bought at the Honey and Herb Shoppe.

I felt compelled to say something. "We don't know for sure what happened to Isabelle yet, Bill. But I really don't think she danced her way off the terrace. I have faith that you didn't hurt her in any way. Isabelle had a problem with people. I'm afraid it may have finally come back on her."

"Regardless of what happened, I've decided to rid myself of my elf magic before I hurt anyone else," Bill declared.

That dragged Manny into the conversation. "How do you propose to do that?"

"I've heard of a woman here at the Village who can help me."

"Who's that?" I asked.

"I'm not sure of her name, but she stays over there in the tent by the Main Gate."

Manny nodded. "The fortune teller."

I'd had a few encounters with Madame Lucinda. I didn't know if she could do what Bill was asking for, but she was a curious resident. Since I wasn't sure what harm it could do to have her say she'd removed his elf magic, I agreed to the plan.

"I'll go with you and introduce you to Madame Lucinda," I offered. "Maybe she can help you."

He smiled broadly as he finished a honey cookie. "Thank you, Jessie. You've been a good friend to me."

"Just one thing I'd like to know," I said to him. "Why does your magic work so strongly with some people and not with others? I'm wearing sandals you made, but I haven't felt the urge to dance out of the museum."

"I don't really know. It's not like my family talks about

the particulars. We all know we have elf magic, and that's that. I think what happens is a connection between me and the person wearing my shoes. Maybe that person has magic of their own."

I thought about it. "Maybe that's it. I certainly have no claim to any particular magic. I hope Madame Lucinda can set your mind at ease."

We went back to the museum where the lines to see Bill's boots were as long as ever. I felt the first warning of a storm on the way at about three p.m. when clouds started blowing in from the ocean.

It didn't take long before rain was sweeping in from the Atlantic, with frequent lightning flashes and jarring claps of thunder. The wind rose, pulling at support lines for tents and vendor's carts. Chase had to close down the climbing wall by three-thirty. The Village had mostly emptied out by four. A few holdouts stuck around to see if the weather would change. They took shelter in the museum and other covered spots.

By closing time at six p.m. the cobblestones were bare of visitors and residents. The sky boiled furiously above us. There were no hurricane warnings up, but the coming evening was vicious enough to keep everyone indoors.

I'd closed the museum at five when the last of the visitors had fled toward the Main Gate. Manny put on a huge poncho and rode to his apartment on his bicycle. Bill and I met Chase at the Monastery Bakery where he was trying to help with a squabble among the monks. There was always some disagreement between the hooded Brotherhood of the Sheaf, the only unpaid workers in the Village. They were only there for the love of the Renaissance.

I didn't ask what was going on. The mutinous faces of Brother Carl, who was technically the monks' leader, and Brother John who coveted his position, were enough to keep me out of it.

"We're going to see Madame Lucinda," I told Chase. "Bill wants her help to get rid of his elf magic."

Chase nodded. He was seated on a rough table listening to the monks complain about someone not adhering to the strict baking code they maintained. "I'll probably be here a while. Stop by when you're done. Maybe you can rescue me from hearing anymore about what kind of flour they need to use."

I smiled and quickly kissed him. "Cheer up. Maybe you can keep them from holding a midnight bake-off to decide what action they should take. You know they'd want you to be the judge."

He groaned. "Don't remind me. Good luck."

Bill and I shared a big umbrella to walk from the bakery to the fortuneteller's tent. We walked past the entrance to Sherwood Forest. It was five acres of trees and rocks where Robin Hood and his Merry Men and Women lived and worked.

Robin, Friar Tuck, and a new Maid Marion, were talking with potential forest folk who'd waited through the storm for a crack at becoming part of their band. Despite the torrential downpour, it seemed that Robin was requiring his recruits to start a fire as part of their aptitude test. The small group of young men and women were doing their best, but it appeared to be a hopeless task. Robin saluted as he saw Bill and me walk by.

I was so glad I was over my fascination with the forest.

Despite the howling winds and rain, Madame Lucinda's purple tent didn't so much as shudder. It looked as though it would've been blown away by the storm, but there it was.

Madame Lucinda really did have some kind of magic. I couldn't speculate on what kind it was, but it seemed to involve dragons. To put it flatly, I was fairly sure that the woman was part dragon herself. And there was the matter of a small dragon living with her.

Other people, including Chase, claimed not to see it. Maybe Bill could if he really had elf magic as he claimed. I wasn't sure why I could see it.

I pulled on Bill's sleeve before we went inside the tent. I

had to yell for him to hear me over the rain and wind. "Are you sure about this? Once your magic is gone, you might not be able to get it back."

"I'm sure." He pushed his wet hair off his forehead. I noticed that his hand trembled as he did it. "I'm done with this stupid heritage." He lifted the purple and gold tent flap.

"Okay." I followed him in, wondering if he'd be able to see Madame Lucinda's wonders as I could. He'd said he could see Wanda, another thing Chase couldn't see. I was excited to find out.

Once the tent flap fell behind us, there was no sound from the storm outside. The tent walls didn't move with the wind buffeting them. It was as though inside the tent was sheltered from everything outside.

"Lady Jessie." Madame Lucinda bowed her head respectfully to me. "To what do I owe the honor of your visit?"

She was deeply stooped, with wild gray hair. Her face didn't show her age to be more than possibly forties or early fifties. Her body appeared much older. She always wore a long purple robe. From the waist up, she seemed to be a normal human, but the bottom part of her was abnormally large and out of proportion to the rest of her.

I remembered why that was from the first time I'd seen her without her robe. Her legs were thick and scaly, and there was a wide tail too. It made me swallow hard thinking about it.

"Madame Lucinda." I bowed my head in return. "This is Bill Warren."

She nodded. "The cobbler. Yes. I've seen your work. Very nice. What can I do for you?"

Bill was really nervous too. His voice was barely above a whisper. He had to clear his throat to be heard. "Jessie tells me you might be able to take away my elf magic."

Her eyes were bright as they focused on his face. "You realize what will happen if I take away your magic?"

"Yes." He looked at me. "No. Probably not. I've always

had it. I inherited it from my father and his father before him."

"Yes. I know."

"Wait." I glanced between them. "He really has elf magic?"

"Of course. It runs through his bloodline. No doubt from an ancestral mating of human and elf." She shrugged one shoulder. "It happens."

"You mean there really are elves?"

"Not so much as there once were, Jessie," she explained. "But there are still elves in many uninhabited areas of the world."

"Elves—like tiny little men who make toys and cookies?" I couldn't believe it. Wait until I tell Chase.

"No. Elves are another race, and they are about the same size as humans." She smiled as though I were a small child. "Perhaps you're thinking of another race of magical beings."

"Perhaps." I felt a little stupid with the way she said it.

Her sharp eyes turned back to Bill. "Losing your magic will mean that your work will be good, but without that indefinable spark that people so admire. There could be other complications for you as well. Magic changes everything. When yours is gone, your life will be different."

Bill seemed to think if over and then finally made up his mind. "I don't care. Whatever it is, it will be better than harming the people who buy my shoes."

"Wait! Wait just a minute." I pointed to the small green dragon that was lounging on Madame Lucinda's fortune telling table. Occasionally its bright gold eyes would blink and its tail would swish like a cat's. "Can you see Buttercup on the table over there?" I asked Bill.

He followed my gaze and stared intently as the terrier-sized dragon got up and stretched. "Yikes." He took a step back. "Is that real? Or is this another Ren Faire thing?"

I did a little touchdown dance. "Yes! Someone besides me can see the dragon."

"Buttercup is very real." Madame Lucinda stroked her

pet's back ridge. "Only a special few can see her."

"Wow!" Bill exclaimed. "I thought they were extinct."

"They aren't dinosaurs," I told him. "They're supposed to be mythological creatures like centaurs and unicorns. They aren't supposed to exist."

"I guess I can see her because of my magic," he said.

"That's right," Madame Lucinda agreed. "That will change if I take it."

"I know. But I can't control it. And after Isabelle's death, I don't want it anymore. Please." He bowed his head. "Take it."

Bill looked as though he was braced for a flash of painful lightning that would end his elf magic. His body was hunched and stiff, eyes closed and fists clenched.

Madame Lucinda blinked her eyes. "It is gone."

He moved around a little. "Is that it?"

"That is a great deal." She stared deeply into his eyes. "I will hold your magic for three days and three nights. During that time, you may return and claim it. After the third night, I will disperse it into the universe. Good luck, Mr. Warren."

Bill was happy enough about it. Madame Lucinda's voice had held notes of doom in it. Bill skipped out of the tent with a big grin on his face. He was laughing as the tent flap closed behind him.

I turned to her. "He's going to be miserable without it, isn't he?"

"I should think so. Perhaps his commitment to be without magic will see him through."

"Why can I see Buttercup? I don't have elf magic. I don't understand."

She smoothed a slightly scaly hand across my cheek. "Which is what makes you so wonderful."

"Wonderful? Do I have some kind of magic too?"

"Only you can answer that question."

I really hate those kinds of answers.

Chapter Eleven

The storm was still raging across the Village. So much rain had fallen that large puddles had begun to accumulate across the cobblestones and grass. I held on to my umbrella and thought about magic all the way back to the Dungeon.

Bill was long gone by the time I got outside the tent. I hoped he wouldn't be too unhappy without his magic. I needed him to finish the exhibit at the museum.

Magic. I was tossing the word around as lightly as though I was saying pretzel or skirt.

I believed in magic. Our home had been changed by it when a sorcerer had passed through the Village. But I couldn't see magic in myself. I wasn't sure about Bill's ex-magic—although he had been able to see Wanda and Buttercup.

Chase was drying off and changing clothes when I got back. "I have to go back out," he told me. "I thought I was in for the night, but then D'Amos called. The storm stampeded the camels out of their pen. We're going to round them up."

"I won't bother changing then so I can go with you."

"Or there might be something else you should do." He pulled on a dry shirt.

"Yeah? Like what?"

"I saw Tony while I was at the Monastery Bakery." He grinned. "Your brother wants to be a monk."

"My brother? A monk? You've gotta be kidding."

"Nope. He's going through the acceptance process tonight. That was part of the problem at the bakery. I resolved it for now, but it will be back again with Tony taking his vows."

I flopped down on the bed. "I'd rather herd camels than try to talk him out of it."

"That's up to you. I thought you should know."

I sighed. Heavily. My twin brother Tony had spent as much time at the Village as I had. He'd done as many things in the Village as I had. His last job had been working for Robin Hood doing online promotion. I'd hoped it would be his last job for a while. I was doomed to disappointment.

Still, he was my brother and the only one left in my family. Our parents had been killed in a wreck when we were very young. Our grandmother had taken us in, but she was gone now too. We only had each other. There wasn't anyone else who could talk Tony out of doing something stupid.

Chase finished dressing and put on his poncho and boots. "I'll see you later. Don't let your brother become a monk. Love you."

He kissed me and was gone. He knew I'd go get Tony and save the monks. That's why he'd told me.

Argh!

I put on my knee-high rubber boots after carefully putting away the sandals Bill had made for me in Tennessee. I couldn't feel any magic in them. I jiggled them around in my hands. Nothing.

I hadn't wanted to dance off a terrace or run down stairs since I'd put them on. It seemed to me that if I had magic, as Madame Lucinda had hinted, that I'd be able to feel something from them.

I finally shrugged and put on my rain poncho too. It was going to be a long night.

* * *

The Brotherhood of the Sheaf was a unique group of people who'd lived in the Village since it was created. They'd built the Monastery Bakery to serve their bread which was the focal point for their physical and spiritual lives. They took their ideas from the concept of bread being the staff of life.

There were usually around twenty five to thirty monks. Each year, new men came and went. They didn't fill the ranks until someone was gone. I had to assume that a monk had left the fold and somehow they'd managed to recruit Tony.

But the monks in their black and brown hooded robes were nothing like my brother. I wasn't sure if he even knew the meaning of the word chaste. He'd been in and out of trouble our whole lives—usually with me bailing him out.

I was really hoping we were past all that since we were in our thirties. It looked like I was wrong.

Tony was my fraternal twin. We looked a lot alike. Both of us were six feet tall and had brown hair. I had blue eyes and he had brown. Our personal statistics looked better on him than they did on me. Girls had loved him since he was twelve. Nothing had happened to change that. I was wondering what he planned to do about that aspect of his life if he became a monk.

The Village seemed very dark, the rain still swamping us. The tiny lamps in the shops and houses didn't seem to reach out with their usual friendly glow like they did on clear nights. It was getting foggy too. Wisps of it obscured the Field of Honor and the houses and shops on the other side of the King's Highway. Chase, D'Amos, and their helpers were in for a rough time trying to get the camels together.

I still envied them their job over mine.

The Monastery Bakery was well lit from the inside. A

giant cartoon figure of a monk holding a loaf of bread under his arm watched from the steep roof as I knocked on the door. A young monk answered immediately.

"I'd like to see my brother, Tony," I told him.

He regarded me with great suspicion. "Tony is not a full brother as yet, my lady. Perhaps you could return later."

"I think you misunderstand me. Tony Morton is really my brother—as in, he and I had the same parents. I'd like to see him right now."

The young man moved to block the door as I would have pushed it aside and gone in. "I'm sorry, my lady. You may not enter this night."

I didn't know what was going on in the bakery, but I could hear chanting and smelled baking bread. I hoped I wasn't too late. The idea of Tony as a full-fledged monk lent impatience to my next move.

The young man was barely five feet tall, and he was scrawny at that. I pushed myself up to my full six feet, and glared down at him. "Have you heard the stories about my broadsword? Men refer to it as one of the Furies. I don't want to hurt you, Brother, but I am going to speak with Tony now."

I could see the panic in his blue eyes. He was uncertain if facing me would be worse than letting down his brothers. I took advantage of his weakness and pushed past him into the bakery. He dropped to the floor, begging me not to go any further.

"What is going on out here?" Brother Carl, the current head of the order, came to the door. "My Lady Jessie! How may I serve you?"

"I didn't come for coffee or pastries," I told him. "I want to see Tony before he takes his vows."

"Brother Tony is working at the oven, which you know is the sacred duty and obligation of all the monks. Tonight, when his bread has risen, he will take his vows."

"Not before I talk to him."

Carl stubbornly maintained his stance in front of me.

"Come on. This is Tony we're talking about, Carl. I can't imagine why you'd want him or why he'd want to be here, but you should re-think this. I've never known him to be without a woman in his bed for more than a day or two. Is that the kind of reputation you want? Think about how it will impact the other new monks you're taking in tonight."

"I know you mean well, Lady Jessie. But your brother has changed. He has assured us of his intention to be chaste."

"He's been chased his whole life—and he's never said no. Let me talk to him, Brother Carl, before it's too late."

Carl finally came around and led me to the area where the big stone ovens were located. It was sweltering in the airless room. Tony took advantage of it. He was the only monk tending an oven without a stitch of clothes on his lean body.

"Brother Tony!" Carl scolded. "We do not remove our robes when we are doing the sacred baking."

Tony looked down at himself as though it hadn't really occurred to him that he was naked. "It was so hot in here. I couldn't breathe. Hi, Sis."

"Put some clothes on." I looked away.

He quickly slid into one of the coarse brown robes. "There. Better? What are you doing here, Jessie?"

"I came to protect you and the brotherhood." I glanced at Brother Carl. "Could we have a minute to talk?"

"Certainly. Brother Tony, take Lady Jessie to your room."

I followed Tony to his tiny, closet-like room. There was a chest and a small bed. I was pretty sure he couldn't fit on the bed. I knew each of the monks had a room like this one.

"What are you doing?" I asked as soon as the door was closed behind us. "You're not exactly monk material."

"Brother Carl thinks I am."

"Brother Carl thinks everyone is monk material. Don't flatter yourself. What happened to working on internet promotion for Robin Hood?"

He shrugged. "I just got tired of hanging around in the

tree houses, you know? Like you did, I guess. Only I didn't fall into a good marriage with the wealthy Bailiff. I don't want to leave the Village. I had to go somewhere."

"Tony, you know you don't want to be a monk! You don't like getting up early in the morning, and I don't believe you're going to give up women."

"You should've hired me to help you at the museum instead of Manny. I needed a break. I could've done what he does."

I knew that wasn't true. I also knew I couldn't make Tony pay attention to me. He would be just as likely to ignore me and the museum. Manny was a much better assistant.

"I'm sorry. I don't think we could work together. But there's a big hiring opportunity right now. Take advantage of it. You could be anyone."

He smirked. "Except a monk, right, Jessie?"

"That's all I wanted to say to you. We both know this is a mistake. You'll ruin the reputation of the brotherhood."

He held up his thumb. "Thanks for the vote of confidence, Sis. I guess we'll find out, won't we?"

The young monk who answered the bakery door ran into the room. "Your bread is burning, Brother Tony. You must come at once."

We followed him back to the oven room. Brother Carl was taking Tony's bread out of the stone oven with a long-handled wood paddle. He placed the loaf next to the others that had just been baked. Tony's loaf was flat and black. It couldn't have looked any worse if he had tried.

"We must have a discussion about your bread making skills, Brother," Carl told him. "Goodnight, Lady Jessie."

"Goodnight." I glanced back at Tony before I left. Hopefully this would help him see that he wasn't meant to be a monk. I left behind the smell of burned bread and went back out into the night.

The rain had stopped, and the wind was dying down. It seemed so quiet in the Village after the storm. I could see some damage from the high wind and heavy rain. Banners were torn down—including the one at the museum. A few pieces of scenery had been blown over. The maintenance crew was going to have their hands full before the Village opened in the morning.

I heard soft murmurs from around the darkened corner of the hatchet-throwing game. It sounded like two lovers having a tryst. I didn't want to intrude and walked past the spot quickly. As I was trying to ignore them, Sir Dwayne emerged from the shadows with Rita Martinez. Her hair was mussed and her bodice askew.

No doubt what's going on there.

The lovers were probably nervous about their rendezvous so they'd left the castle. I hoped they'd talked to the police and explained what had happened to Sir Dwayne, but it wasn't exactly my problem either.

Rita lifted her chin as she passed me on the cobblestones. "Good evening, Lady Jessie."

Sir Dwayne swept past without a word, the lingering aroma of sandalwood following him.

Chase was waiting for me back at the Dungeon. He was dirty and smelly, but victorious. "We got all the camels back where they belong. I thought maybe Wanda was responsible—like she was with the elephants a few months back. But there was a fault in the fence that the camels found. D'Amos and his people are repairing it."

He came to bed after showering. I told him about Tony's decision to become a monk. I didn't think he'd ever stop laughing.

"Why doesn't he apply for one of the open positions?" he asked.

"That's what I said." I didn't mention my brother's remark about me marrying Chase. The two weren't especially close anyway. I didn't want any hard feelings between them.

"You have to let him find his own way, Jessie. It takes some people a little longer than others."

I changed the subject, which was one we never agreed on. Chase hadn't grown up as Tony and I had. He would never understand why it was harder for Tony. Or why I always felt guilty about him when things were going well in my life.

I asked him how training with the knights went. He said they seemed to be a good group.

"Katharina is going to be the star of the show," he said. "She deserves it. She takes more chances and works harder than anyone else."

"Great." I tried to sound enthusiastic about Katharina. My lack of excitement over her prowess was only my own sour grapes. Some part of me still wished I could ride in the joust as a knight.

"You know you could still be a knight," he said again as though reading my mind.

"Not now. I don't have time. It was just something I wanted to do a long time ago." I kissed him. "Thanks for offering. I'm pretty sure I couldn't get through your training anyway. I've heard the knights talking about you. It wasn't pleasant."

He laughed. "But they're the best because of me. That's what counts."

We finally fell asleep in each other's arms. I thought it was morning when I heard his radio go off. It was only three a.m.

"Chase, we need you at the Merry Mynstrel's Stage. Rita Martinez has been attacked."

Chapter Twelve

I got dressed as Chase did, throwing on some denim shorts, boots, and a tank top.

"Why are you going?" he asked.

"I don't like the current trend. You might need someone to watch your back."

"Or you're just nosy about what's going on."

"And Rita is my friend. You know that. Maybe there's something I can do to help."

"Okay. But it could take a while."

"That's fine." I watched him finish dressing and tying back his braid. "Are you asking me not to go?"

"No, of course not." He kissed me and grabbed my hand. "Come on."

Rita had probably ended up at the Merry Mynstrel's Stage on her way back to the castle with Sir Dwayne. If he was the one who'd attacked Rita, this might be the link the police needed to tie Isabelle's death to him too.

Two women from the castle, both romantically involved

with him. It sounded like some kind of pattern to me. Although Sir Dwayne would have to be crazy or stupid to hurt Rita so soon after Isabelle's death.

Chase and I ran across the King's Highway and the Village Green where sprinklers were on despite the rain. I barely missed being drenched in them.

Detective Almond and several of his officers were already at the stage. Chase and I watched as paramedics loaded Rita on a stretcher into the back of an ambulance. Dozens of Village residents were also watching the early morning scene. The bright stadium lights had been switched on. They illuminated the concern on everyone's faces to find another violent crime happening so soon after Isabelle's death.

"Hope we didn't wake you up, Bailiff," Detective Almond snickered.

"What happened?" Chase ignored his sarcasm.

"It looks like another woman from the castle was attacked. I know Rita." He glanced at me. "Maybe her illusive boyfriend who was also Isabelle Franklin's lover did this. I had the paramedics put plastic bags over her hands to preserve any evidence. She fought her attacker."

"How is she?" I questioned.

"She's in bad shape." Detective Almond consulted his notebook. "She looks like someone hit her in the head a few times—maybe with a baseball bat—and then roughed her up. Contusions. Broken bones. We'll see after she gets the once-over at the hospital."

I hated to point the finger at anyone for such a terrible crime, but I couldn't keep silent. "I saw her a few hours ago with Sir Dwayne. They were at the hatchet-throwing game."

Detective Almond wrote in his book. "The same man you were helping her try to protect, right? Funny how these things come back to us, Jessie. If it was, he's a fast worker— already moving on to the next woman."

"They weren't arguing or anything. I think they were kissing." I shrugged.

"Thanks. Maybe you and Rita should've thought Sir Dwayne might not be such a good guy, huh? I suppose they were on their way back to the castle." He scanned the unusually bright landscape.

"Maybe." I felt bad because I knew Rita had worked so hard to protect Sir Dwayne. She had such faith in him. But I had to acknowledge that Detective Almond could be right, and Sir Dwayne didn't deserve her protection.

"What about the shoemaker with magic? Where is he?"

"I don't know. Probably asleep at Fred's house. You could check on him."

"I will." Detective Almond nodded to one of the uniformed officers at his side. The officer grabbed another man, and they walked quickly toward Fred's house.

I hoped Bill was at home asleep. Maybe that would finally quell any questions about his guilt.

"You aren't saying that about Sir Dwayne because it could get your shoemaker off the hook, are you?" Detective Almond asked me.

"No. I'm sure I'm not the only person who saw Rita and Sir Dwayne together. I wouldn't do that anyway."

Detective Almond told Chase he needed his security guards to watch the area as the crime scene team collected evidence of what had happened to Rita. Chase told him he'd stay there while they worked.

At least a dozen Village residents stood around in their pajamas talking about what had happened. Susan Halifax, the harpist from the Merry Mynstrel's Stage, was discussing buying mace or a Taser with a few pirates from the Queen's Revenge. None of them had seen what had happened to Rita.

Most were just worried about who was next.

Chase told everyone to go home. "There's nothing else to see. Everyone is going to be exhausted tomorrow if you don't get some sleep. I'll let you know when the police have some idea of what happened."

There was a lot of muttering, but everyone started to go back to their homes.

Detective Almond pulled me aside. "This Sir Dwayne lives at the castle, right? We didn't see any sign of him when we searched the passageways—unless that was his shirt."

"His position might be a bit shaky with Isabelle gone. I don't think he's been at the Village for long. Are you going to question him?"

"I think that would be a good idea if I can find him, don't you?"

"Sure." I knew he was making fun of me. "I was just trying to help Rita, you know."

"Yeah. I know. But this is what comes of messing around in police business, Jessie. By the way, what were you doing out so late?"

"My brother Tony was about to take his vows as a Brother of the Sheaf."

He held up his hand. "Enough said. Those guys are crazy. Always have been. Who'd live here and not get paid? I'll let Chase know what Sir Dwayne has to say. Thanks."

I was impressed that he'd thanked me so politely. That didn't always happen.

I told Chase I'd see him later. I loved him, but I didn't want to hang around watching the police work all night. Yawning, I headed toward the Dungeon.

It was hard to believe that Sir Dwayne would be stupid enough to throw Isabelle off her terrace and then turn around and attack Rita. He had to know he was on Detective Almond's suspect list. Maybe he couldn't control himself.

That was scary to think about.

"So what do you think really happened?" Wanda appeared at my side as I passed the Hands of Time clock shop.

"You must know already." I hoped she did and would spill it.

"I missed it." Her naked, blue form passed right through a trashcan. "I was watching some of the handsome new knights while they undressed. I was hoping one of them might be able to see me. I had a little dalliance in mind. It's easier when they can see me too."

"That's too bad. It would be nice to get the right person out of the Village before anyone else gets hurt."

"This should get your cobbler off the hook anyway. With the police going after Sir Dwayne, you don't have as much to worry about. Except, of course, for him giving up his magic."

"He didn't really have elf magic," I explained. "The things that happened were coincidences, I'm sure."

"Then why did you take him to the dragon lady? Why ask her to take away his magic if he didn't have any in the first place?"

Wanda couldn't get inside Madame Lucinda's tent, but she could hear plenty from people as they went in and out.

"He wanted to get rid of his magic." I shrugged. "I helped him. Not because I thought he really had magic, but because he was so unhappy about it."

"I see. A mere psychological ploy then."

"What about Isabelle's death?" I thought I might as well ask. "Did you see who killed her?"

"No, blast it!" Wanda's blue face was disappointed. "I would've liked to see Isabelle's face as she was falling. I never liked that little minx. Always looking for the next man she could steal. She and I crossed paths a few times through the years."

We finally crossed the cobblestones and reached the Dungeon. Wanda had been forbidden to enter my home by the sorcerer who'd built it. He'd owed me a favor, and this was his way of repaying it.

"I guess this is it." I tried not to smile smugly, but I couldn't stop myself. Wanda had almost ruined my relationship with Chase before we were married. It was a relief that she couldn't go inside.

"Jessie? I was wondering why you're allowing Chase to spend so much time with that red-haired tart on the horse. Have you no sense of survival? The girl is at least ten years younger than you. I think you overestimate your charms."

"I think you're jealous and would do or say anything to break us up."

"Perhaps." Her face took on an ugly, sly quality. "But then, why is the new knight waiting inside the Dungeon for Chase? Ponder that, dearie."

Wanda was gone with her usual cackle. I thought for a moment that she was lying just to get a reaction from me, but when I opened the door to the Dungeon to go inside, there was Katharina.

"Where's Chase?" she demanded.

Chapter Thirteen

I'd tried really hard not to be jealous of Katharina. She was younger, beautiful, great body, awesome hair. And she was spending quality time with my husband.

I knew that didn't mean that he was cheating with her or that she was even interested in him that way. Still, it was hard to see her there at the steps to our apartment and not be uneasy.

I plastered a big smile on my face. If she was interested in Chase, she wouldn't see that it bothered me at all. And I wouldn't give him up without a fight! "Hello, Katharina. Chase is working. Can I do something for you?"

"No. I'll find him later." She started to leave.

"Why did you come here looking for him at this time of night?"

"Because my horse is sick. I don't know what to do. I thought Chase might be able to help."

She started to push open the door.

"Chase is working at a crime scene, but I can help you. We can find D'Amos. He'll know what to do or who to call."

I was at my helpful, cheerful best.

"Why would you help me? I've heard a lot of people talking about how much you hate me and that you think I'm trying to steal Chase from you."

I faced her. "And are you?"

She smiled, flicked her hair, and pushed her breasts out. "I would if I could. Chase is everything I've ever wanted in a man—and he looks great in his armor. But there's no way he'll look at me. All he talks about is horses, jousting moves, and you, Jessie. He's totally crazy about you."

I tried not to sigh or act in any way as though I was relieved by her words. But I felt pretty good about her confession. Of course Chase was in love with me. I never doubted our love, or him.

Or at least I hadn't doubted it much.

"Let's go find D'Amos," I encouraged as I opened the door. "He'll know what to do for your horse. If it makes you feel any better, Chase would do the same thing. He loves horses, but he's not a vet."

"All right." She carefully inclined her head. "Thank you, Lady Jessie."

"Just Jessie. Do you go by Kate or Kat sometimes?"

"No. Just Katharina. Someday I hope to be Lady Katharina because of my daring exploits as a knight and jouster. Is that how you got your title?"

"It's a long story," I told her. "We'll talk on the way."

D'Amos wasn't awake or ready for visitors, but he graciously dressed and accompanied us to the stables to take a look at Katharina's horse. I hadn't realized that Katharina had received special permission to bring her own horse to ride on the Field of Honor.

Something else Chase hadn't mentioned.

I could see the stadium lights were still on at the other side of the Village so I knew Chase and the police were still working. I hoped Rita would recover as I walked with D'Amos and Katharina, not really listening to their conversation about the horse and its symptoms.

Thinking about Rita made me think about Sir Dwayne. From what Rita had confided—and seeing Sir Dwayne chastised by Isabelle—maybe it was possible he was the killer. Maybe Rita had confronted him about it and he'd lashed out at her. It would make sense in a terrible way.

I didn't know much about him, but he'd always struck me as being a bully. Look how he'd been with Bill at the museum. He hadn't been at the Village long. And maybe I was wrong for feeling that way about him. I knew Bill faced problems being new here too. I didn't want to be quick to judge just because I didn't know him.

It must be nice to be like Detective Almond and absolutely know for sure—even when you're wrong—that you're right.

We'd reached the stables with their particular pungent odor. The horses were unsettled by the storm and D'Amos switching on the light. We walked to the stall where Katharina's horse was being kept. The poor chestnut stallion lay on the hay-covered floor, not moving.

"Can you help him?" she asked D'Amos.

He knelt down close to the animal. "Let me take a look at him. If I can't help, we have a vet on call for the Village. He takes care of most of our animals."

Katharina wasn't sure about that. "Foxfire is an Arabian thoroughbred. I don't know if I trust him to some vet who takes care of goats and elephants."

D'Amos moved his hands carefully over the large horse. "That's up to you, but he's a mighty fine vet. I trusted him when I was the director of the zoo in Columbia, and I trust him now."

She nodded. "I guess that's okay then. What do you think is wrong with Foxfire?"

He didn't respond as he checked the horse. I sat on a nearby bale of hay and watched them talk to the horse as D'Amos listened to Foxfire's heart and checked him for other problems.

I'd brought my cell phone with me. I wasn't working,

and thought I might need it. Some days it was weird even having one because I used it so rarely. It rang a few minutes later when Chase got back to the Dungeon and couldn't find me.

I explained the situation about Katharina's horse to him. "I knew you'd get D'Amos so that's what we did."

"Do you need me to come up there?"

"No. I think you've done enough for one night. Get some rest. I'll be back as soon as I can."

"Okay. Thanks, Jessie. I told you Katharina wasn't so bad."

I didn't mention her moment of stark honesty with me. There was no need to keep the bad blood going between us. I wanted Chase to know that I trusted him. I hoped I could always feel that way.

The sky was turning light as I left D'Amos and Katharina at the stables with Foxfire. D'Amos had called the Village vet and remained there when he'd arrived. Katharina was questioning every move they made as the poor horse was examined.

I'd finally decided there was nothing more I could do to help. I might still be able to get back to sleep for a while. I hoped Chase had been able to get some sleep. I wished I could find a good second-in-command for him too. It was an idea worth contemplating.

The maintenance people were already up and moving around the Village to get repairs done early. Branches were littering the cobblestones. Almost everything that hadn't been nailed down had blown somewhere it didn't belong. I noticed that the Kelli's Kites sign had blown down. It was on top of the Frenchy's Fudge roof. The fountains were filled with debris. It looked like a big job.

I was glad I didn't have to do it.

My brain was on autopilot as I walked into the Dungeon. All I was thinking about was snuggling up to Chase in bed before he had to go back to work. The image made me almost walk right into another person waiting in the lower

Dungeon where the fake prisoners moaned and complained during the day.

I stopped short, thinking that we needed to start locking the outside door as well as our apartment door. Then I realized who was hiding there. "Sir Dwayne?"

Chapter Fourteen

He put his hand across my mouth and brought me close to him, a small gun between us. "Quiet. The police are looking for me. I knew they wouldn't come here because this is where the Bailiff lives. "

I made a few snuffling sounds since I couldn't actually speak. Chase was in the apartment, but there was no way to let him know what was going on.

"I figure I'll hold out here until ten when the Main Gate opens and then I can sneak out in the crowd."

It was a good plan. With all the actors trying out for parts and thousands of visitors streaming into the Village, the police would have a hard time spotting Sir Dwayne. I'd noticed that he'd changed clothes. Instead of his usual elegant raiment that routinely matched what Isabelle wore, he was wearing street clothes—jeans and a Myrtle Beach T-shirt.

"You showing up is actually a benefit. The police will be looking for one man, not a couple. You don't mind going out of the Village with me, do you?"

His blue eyes stared into mine. He kept his hand on my
mouth. I nodded my head to let him know leaving with him
was fine. I started looking around for anything I could use as
a weapon. If I could stun him, I could probably get away.

My cell phone rang. It was Chase—I had a special
ringtone for him—Chapel of Love by the Dixie Cups.

I realized that Chase wouldn't think anything of not
being able to reach me since he knew I was with D'Amos at
the stables. He'd go about whatever was in store for him that
morning, maybe try to call again on a break. He wouldn't
even question it until I was gone with Sir Dwayne.

It was a sobering thought. I could be miles away by then.

Sir Dwayne took my cell phone from my pocket and
smiled when he saw Chase's face on the screen. "You're the
Bailiff's girl, huh? That's interesting."

I tried to tell him that I was Chase's wife, but it sounded
more like mumbo jumbo. The screen went dark. Chase was
probably up and getting ready to go out.

"Maybe we better go a little further into the Dungeon.
We don't want the Bailiff to see us before I can get out of the
Village."

Sir Dwayne was surprisingly strong. I wouldn't have
thought so since I'd pegged him as a dandy with his fine silk
clothes and elegant demeanor. I could tell by the way he held
on to me as he dragged me to the back of the Dungeon that
he could've easily lifted Isabelle and thrown her over the
edge of the terrace.

The cells in the Dungeon were made of flimsy material.
Keeping them together relied more on visitors not wanting to
get too near the sad, disgusting look of the prisoners than any
real foundation.

Sir Dwayne kicked one of the cell doors open and
pushed both of us inside past the prisoner who only called
out for help during the day when the Village was open. The
prisoner watched with frozen eyes as my captor shoved me to
the dirty floor and fell on top of me. His one hand still

covered my mouth, and his other arm held me.

"Let's be quiet now," he whispered. "We wouldn't want to hurt your boyfriend."

I didn't want Chase to be hurt, especially since Sir Dwayne only wanted to escape the Village. I figured we'd hide here until Chase was gone and then I'd sneak out with him. I hoped Sir Dwayne's actions with Rita and Isabelle were only because they had relationships with him. He didn't really know who I was, and it was better to keep it that way.

It was only a few minutes later that Chase came out of our apartment and locked the door behind him. He glanced around the Dungeon area, shrugged, and then turned on the special effects in the prisoners' cells. He probably didn't expect to be back before visitors came through the Main Gate. The Dungeon was a popular stop.

Most of the prisoners didn't move. They called out or cried, begging for someone to help them. Bad lighting played across them making the area seem fearful. Sir Dwayne managed to choose one of the prisoners who moved in his cell. When Chase flipped the switch, our prisoner moved his arms back and forth and turned his head from side to side.

Sir Dwayne and I obstructed the prisoner from his movements. The prisoner began making an uncharacteristic grinding sound because his arms wouldn't move. I held my breath, hoping Chase wouldn't notice.

That didn't happen.

He started with the first of the four cells, searching for the problem. I tried to move out of the way so that the prisoner would start moaning and stop grinding. Sir Dwayne's heavy body made that impossible.

I tried to think what I could do to warn Chase. He'd walk right into Sir Dwayne's gun that he was holding between us. I knew he wouldn't hesitate to shoot Chase. There had to be some way to keep that from happening.

Taking my courage in hand, I opened my mouth and bit down hard on Sir Dwayne's hand as Chase was examining the prisoner in the second cell.

"Bloody hell!" Sir Dwayne moved away from me and nursed his injured fingers. It seemed he wasn't as tough as he was large and strong. "Why did you do that? I don't want to hurt anyone."

"The best way to accomplish that would be to get off my wife." Chase's voice was decisive. "Now."

I could see that Chase was holding a fake sword he'd taken from one of the other prisoners. It was a good ruse. Unless Dwayne kicked or hit the sword and broke it, he probably wouldn't know that it wasn't real.

But Chase couldn't see the gun either. I yelled out a warning and rolled on top of Sir Dwayne. "Get out of the way!"

I tried to grab the small gun. I thought it was too tiny to hurt anyone but I didn't want to take any chances. I heard it go off and immediately thought I'd been hit. Chase grabbed me and got me out of the way. I felt my chest and stomach, but there was no blood.

But blood was oozing from Sir Dwayne's T-shirt where he'd accidentally shot himself. Or I'd shot him? I wasn't sure what that police report would say.

Sir Dwayne was astonished as he looked down at his chest. "She shot me. I can't believe she shot me." He stared at the gun in his hand and then slowly slid to the floor.

Chase helped me up. "Are you okay? Did he hurt you, Jessie?"

"No. I'm fine. He just wanted me to help him escape the Village. I don't think he planned to hurt anyone."

"Except for Rita and Isabelle." He examined Dwayne and then called 911, followed by Detective Almond and then his Village security team.

"Is he dead?" I asked.

"No. He'll be okay. An ambulance is coming. Detective Almond can take care of the rest." Chase put his arms around me. "I'm sorry you got involved with it."

"Me too," I sighed.

Chase was trained as a paramedic to deal with

emergencies before the professionals could arrive. He was applying pressure to Sir Dwayne's gunshot wound when the ambulance arrived. I trusted his judgment that he would be okay.

It wasn't long before I heard sirens. Detective Almond arrived at the same time as the ambulance. He waylaid the paramedics from reaching us. "How serious is the gunshot wound, Manhattan?"

"It was through and through, off to the right side. I don't think it hit anything vital, and it's a small caliber weapon." He held up the bloody bullet he'd found on the floor.

"Good. Let me have a minute with him before they take him."

The paramedics protested, but Detective Almond overrode their decision to get Sir Dwayne and leave immediately for the hospital. He began questioning his prisoner.

"I didn't kill Isabelle, and I didn't hurt Rita," Sir Dwayne said loudly. "You're all my witnesses. I'm not admitting to something I didn't do. I want a lawyer!"

"What happened here?" Detective Almond scanned the make-believe jail cell with distaste.

"He took Jessie hostage to get out of the Village," Chase said. "They struggled with his gun, and it went off, wounding him."

"So you're not guilty of anything, Dwayne? Is that right?" Detective Almond summed it up. "But you're carrying a gun and tried to force this woman to accompany you out of the Village. Those aren't exactly the actions of an innocent man."

Sir Dwayne looked frantic. "Please. I don't want to die. I didn't do anything."

"Then why try to sneak out holding my wife hostage?" Chase asked.

"I thought maybe no one would recognize me. I knew when the police were questioning me yesterday that I was gonna get shafted. Someone saw me with Rita before she was attacked. I stopped at a pub, and she went back to the castle. That's the last I saw of her."

"What pub?" Chase asked.

"Baron's." Sir Dwayne closed his eyes, obviously in pain. "Can I go to the hospital now?"

"You certainly can," Detective Almond said. "Just know that I'll be there to charge you with murder, assault, kidnapping, and whatever else I can find when you wake up. I'll be the first face you see."

He waved the paramedics in to take care of Sir Dwayne. They were a little huffy about having to wait, but in a few minutes they had their patient on a stretcher and were walking out the Dungeon door with him.

"Do you want me to check with Baron's to see if Sir Dwayne's story is true?" Chase asked.

"No. I think we got the man we're looking for. What are they going to tell you at the pub? He was there, but they weren't sure what time? I'll get a statement from him when he comes back from surgery. We'll see then." Detective Almond nodded at me. "Jessie, come to the station later today and file charges against Dwayne. Someone will take your statement."

I nodded, but I wasn't sure I wanted to file charges against him. Yes, he'd lost it, but I didn't blame him for being desperate. Who wouldn't have been in his place? I didn't want to add to the murder charge he was facing. Was that crazy?

Chase wouldn't agree when I told him. I was sure of that. And maybe I was wrong not to file charges. Sir Dwayne could have shot me or Chase.

But he didn't.

I hoped the police had the right man now, but it could as easily have been my shoemaker being charged with murder.

I was just glad it was finally over.

Chapter Fifteen

After everyone was gone, Chase offered to buy me a funnel cake at Fabulous Funnels. I hadn't had one in forever. People were always saying how bad they were for you. I decided I'd have this one with fruit and just a sprinkling of powdered sugar. That way it wouldn't be too bad.

Over funnel cakes Chase asked, "You don't want to file charges against Sir Dwayne, do you?"

"Am I that transparent?"

"To me. I know you always take up for the underdog, Jessie. But I think Detective Almond may have it right this time. Sir Dwayne was Isabelle's lover and seeing Rita on the side. That was dangerous in itself. Isabelle probably found out, and they ended up having the fight everyone heard on the terrace. Not long after she was thrown to the ground."

"I'm not disagreeing that it's possible Dwayne killed Isabelle. But it was only yesterday that Detective Almond thought Bill had killed her. Not to mention that I know what it's like to be accused of doing something you didn't do.

Detective Almond thought I killed Wanda too."

"I agree that he's not always right."

"He'd find his own mother guilty just to get out of the Village."

"That's a little harsh."

"I suppose so." I stabbed a piece of strawberry and funnel cake together. "Shouldn't we at least check with Baron's and see if anyone noticed Dwayne there last night?"

"Exactly what I had in mind."

"If he was lying, and Detective Almond builds a decent case against him, I'll file charges too. Otherwise I feel bad enough that the poor man got shot."

Chase smiled and kissed me. "Okay. Let's see what happens. In the meantime, your shoemaker star is free to make magic shoes at the museum today. The construction crew said his shop should be ready tomorrow."

"Good. I can't wait to tell him. I know that he and Fred will be happy not to be roomies anymore."

We talked about what had happened at the Dungeon and Katharina's horse. Several residents stopped by our table to ask Chase if there was anything new about what had happened to Rita. Mother Goose said a large floral arrangement was being sent from everyone at the Village to the hospital for her. She also asked for money from us to add to what she'd received for the flowers.

"I heard she's regained consciousness and is making a fuss about them letting her go." Mother Goose stroked Phineas' feathers as she spoke. "She's making progress. A bunch of us are going to see her after the Village closes today. Maybe you two should come along."

We agreed that we wanted to see Rita, but Chase couldn't make a commitment to go to the hospital until he saw that he had a clear space in his schedule for the day. I knew I'd wait and go with him.

There was plenty of time to catch a shower and change clothes before the Village opened. I walked with Chase down to Baron's. I loved mornings at the Village when everyone was up and getting ready for the day. The Lovely Laundry Ladies flirted with Chase as they walked by with their baskets of laundry. They heckled visitors and managed to get a few of them to help wash clothes at the well each day.

Not my cup of tea, but male visitors loved getting wet with the buxom ladies.

Mary Shift was opening her doors at Wicked Weaves. Her baskets and other hand woven items were amazing. I'd been her apprentice for a summer. I still had scars on my fingers from being cut by the sweet grass she used to make baskets. She waved and smiled before going inside.

Miss Lolly, as she was known, was bringing in a new crop of fresh lavender to her shop. The breeze blew the scent toward us. I had a lovely lavender wreath in the kitchen that she'd given me and Chase for our wedding.

Some of the residents' children were playing on the Swan Swing near the Frog Catapult. I often wondered if Chase and I would ever have children. We'd talked about it, and both of us thought it would be amazing to have at least one child. The sorcerer had been kind enough to set up a beautiful nursery for us. I just didn't see it happening anytime soon.

"There's Baron now." Chase pointed to the short, round man in a mud brown shirt and britches as he let himself into his establishment. "Let's see what he has to say."

Baron kept to himself more than most in the Village. He actually lived outside—in the real world. I'd heard that he and his wife had tried living above his tavern here but she'd been unhappy. Life at the Ren Faire wasn't for everyone.

"Good morning, Baron," Chase addressed him. "If you have a moment, I'd like to ask you a few questions."

"Of course, Sir Bailiff. You are always welcome here. What information do you need?"

Chase asked if he'd seen Sir Dwayne at his pub last night. Baron nodded. "He was here for a few hours. I'm not sure what time he arrived, but he left as I closed near midnight. He was with Rita Martinez from the castle. Is there a problem?"

"No, good sir." Chase smiled and shook his hand. "Is there anything I may do for you this day?"

Baron frowned a little. "If you could somehow keep that pesky ghost out of here, now that I'd appreciate! Saying as much, I know there is nothing you can do. I have spoken with Tilly Morgenstern who has promised me a spell that will keep Wanda out. I can't see her, mind you. But she wreaks havoc here on a regular basis."

"Is Tilly Morgenstern charging you for this spell?"

"No. We bartered for it. No need to worry, Bailiff. All is well."

Chase nodded to him, and we left the pub.

"So no help there. It was later that Rita was attacked," Chase reminded me as we walked in the sunshine. "We'd need proof of where he was at three a.m. or just before."

"Maybe when Rita is feeling better she'll have some idea of who attacked her." "Let's hope so. What Dwayne did with you was stupid, but doesn't tie him to Rita's attack or Isabelle's murder."

Manny rode by on his tall bicycle. He was still having difficulty stopping it. He ran the front wheel into the wall that surrounded the Village but regained his footing quickly after toppling from it. "Lady Jessie! I went to check in on Bill the cobbler. He is refusing to come to the museum today. What shall I do?"

I smiled at Chase. "I guess this is where we part until lunch. I'll talk to you later."

He put his hand on his chest and bowed to me. "My Lady." Then he swept me off my feet with a wonderful romantic kiss.

All of the local shopkeepers as well as some character actors applauded.

"To make up for the mistaken idea that you and I will ever part," Chase whispered as he put me back on my feet.

I curtsied and laughed at him. "Good sir, I know we shall never say goodbye."

There was more applause and smiles. Everyone in the Village loves gossip, but they love a good romance even more. No one wanted me and Chase to break up. They just wanted to know what was happening—like a large, nosey family.

Chase said he was going to interview people at the castle to see if anyone had noticed Sir Dwayne coming in last night. I left with Manny to find out what was wrong with Bill. I walked, even though Manny offered me a ride on his bicycle.

Fred the Red Dragon lived on the other side of the Village near the Mother Goose Pavilion. I could hear Phineas squawking as he received his morning bath. I knocked at the door to the tiny cottage Fred and Bill were sharing as Manny ran his bike into a privy to stop it and got down.

"You're going to get hurt doing that," I told him as I waited for someone to answer the door.

"I'll get the hang of it," Manny said. "I'm good at these things."

Fred finally answered the door. He was wearing red boxer shorts—and nothing else. "Lady Jessie." He almost fell over trying to bow. "I wasn't expecting you. Please excuse the mess of my abode. It's mostly that stupid shoemaker's fault."

I'd been to Fred's cottage before so I knew better than to think Bill had made it that messy by himself. I walked inside, ignoring the empty pizza boxes and half-eaten plates of spaghetti. "Where's my cobbler?"

Fred scratched his chin. "Was I supposed to be holding that for you? Did the monks send it over from the bakery?"

"My shoemaker." Argh! "Where's Bill?"

Manny walked past Fred, ahead of me. "This way, Lady Jessie. Mind the food on the floor."

He opened a side door off the kitchen and revealed Bill still sleeping and snoring loudly in bed.

"Bill!" I shook him. "Its me, Jessie. You need to wake up. I have good news for you."

He mumbled and turned over.

"He was really drunk last night when he came in," Fred said. "I tried to tell him that it's hard to go to bed at midnight and get up at ten. I've done it. No picnic."

I concentrated on getting Bill out of bed. "Good news. Your shop is going to be ready tomorrow. You can move in. I'll get some knaves and varlets to help you."

He muttered sleepily. "That's good news, Jessie. Thanks. What time is it?"

Manny looked at his impressive gold pocket watch. "Nearly nine a.m., cobbler. You should be up and ready for the day. Lady Jessie has other important things to do besides rousting you from your bed."

"Okay. I'm awake." Bill put his feet on the floor. Manny drew in a quick breath while Fred started laughing.

Bill was naked.

"Leave at once, Lady Jessie." Manny put his hand over my eyes and propelled me out of the bedroom. "I apologize for bringing you here this way. Go on about your business. I shall get the knave up and moving."

What fun would it be to tell him I'd seen naked men before? "Thanks. I'll meet you at the museum."

At the Dungeon, maintenance people were taking a look at the prisoners to see if everything was working after their trauma with Sir Dwayne. The workers said good morning and I waved back.

I made a quick call to the hospital to find out how Rita was doing. The woman at the information desk said she was stable. I asked about Sir Dwayne at the same time. He'd already been treated and released. I was sure Detective Almond would be happy about that.

Showering quickly, I dressed and got ready for the long day ahead.

I looked into the full-length mirror one last time. My headscarf matched the green in my skirt and the embroidery in my vest. I wore a thin, white blouse under the vest, hoping I wouldn't get too hot. I liked the gypsy look. I tucked the small book residents had been given to write up the new recruits into my side pouch, and attached my cup for free drinks to my belt loop.

My cell phone was on the dresser. I turned the sound down and put it in my skirt pocket. It was unlikely anyone from Adventureland would catch me with it, and it made me feel safer after what had happened that morning.

Before I put on the sandals Bill had made for me in Tennessee, I examined them. If there was magic in the leather, it was only the exquisite craftsmanship. Maybe Madame Lucinda was right, and only those with some magic of their own could have the full benefit of Bill's elf magic.

The way Bill's magic seemed to affect people made me glad that I didn't have any. I didn't like the idea of dancing myself to death or falling off a tall structure because I couldn't control my feet.

I was whistling as I locked the apartment door behind me. The workers downstairs were gone. They'd left on the usual lights and sounds from the tortured prisoners. I ignored them as usual and opened the outside door to the Dungeon.

A blast of light hit me in the face and nearly blinded me. I took a step back and covered my face with my hands.

"Be wary this day, Lady Jessie." Madame Lucinda's voice was clear.

I peeked between my fingers. She was standing right outside the doorway—possibly not able to come in because of the sorcerer's spell that kept Wanda out too. "Why? What's wrong?"

"Be wary," she said again.

I finally opened my eyes and, she was gone.

What was that supposed to mean? Why didn't she say something else so that I'd know what to be wary of?

Then I realized that she wasn't even there.

I scanned the cobblestones going in both directions from the Dungeon. There was no sign of her there or in the grass around me. I'd watched her painful movements. She wasn't fast enough to have run away in that time.

Did I have some kind of vision? Or was it a product of

being up most of the night?

I tended to believe it was lack of sleep and too much adrenalin. I'd never experienced anything like it, but then Madame Lucinda was unlike anyone I'd ever met.

I was so busy thinking about it that I didn't notice Katharina until she tapped me on the shoulder.

"Lady Jessie?"

I jumped a few inches. "Oh, it's you. Sorry. I was looking for someone else."

Katharina glanced around. "No one else is here."

"I know. Silly, right? What can I do for you?"

"I just wanted to thank you for your help this morning with my horse. Foxfire is going to be fine. The vet said it wasn't anything serious. He'll be up and jousting in no time."

"I'm so glad. You know, I always wanted to be a knight and joust on the Field of Honor. They didn't have any female knights, and I didn't ask if it was possible. I'm jealous, but so happy it's finally happened."

She smiled at me. "You aren't too old to take your place beside me on the Field of Honor. Maybe you should learn to joust too. I wouldn't mind having some female companionship up there—besides the ladies sighing over the knights."

"Thanks. But handling the museum is all I have time for now. I don't want to give that up. When you ride out there, you'll be taking me with you on Firefox. I can't wait to watch."

She briefly hugged me and yawned. "I'm glad I'm only practicing today. I'm going home to get some sleep."

Lucky Katharina. Sleep didn't seem to be on my to-do list.

The Main Gate would open in fifteen minutes. Flower girls and musicians passed me on their way to welcome the first visitors. A group of the Templar Knights rushed by on horseback from their encampment in the woods behind the Dungeon. All of them were standing on their saddles wielding their curved swords.

There wasn't going to be enough time to ask Madame Lucinda if she'd visited me in spirit at the Dungeon. It would have to wait until everything was set up at the museum and Manny could take over for a few minutes.

I passed Luke Helms at the Jolly Pipemaker's Shoppe. He looked unhappy. I knew there wasn't a lot of time to chat, but hopefully Manny already had Bill up and dressed and on his way to the museum.

"Good morning, sir." I curtsied to him. "How art thou?"

He shook his head. "I forgot to get something for breakfast this morning. Once the gate opens, there won't be time until lunch. My stomach is growling."

I thought about Mrs. Potts and her honey cookies. It wasn't a long walk between the pipe shop and the Honey and Herb Shoppe. I happened to be heading that way. Why not?

Luke and Mrs. Potts would be perfect together. I should have seen it before. Both of them were alone. She wanted someone to care for—he needed someone to take care of him.

"You know, Mrs. Potts always has warm cookies out of the oven by now. I think that would be good for breakfast, don't you?"

He rubbed his worn hands together. "I do, indeed. Thank you, my lady. I'll head down there now."

"I shall walk awhile with you, Sir Pipemaker, if I may."

He held out his arm, and I slipped my hand into it. My mind was filled with crazy ideas about Luke and Mrs. Potts getting together. He was even wearing a blue shirt that reminded me of her blue mobcap. It was a sign!

We were at her shop in no time. I went in her cozy little cottage with him, explaining his plight to my sympathetic friend. "I knew there'd be some cookies ready." I sniffed. "I can tell that I wasn't wrong."

"Bless my soul! You know I always have cookies baking and tea brewing by this time." She shyly smiled at Luke. "Mr. Helms."

"Mrs. Potts." He removed his hat and bobbed his head.

"Oh call me Bea," she said. "And I'll call you Luke."

"Sounds good to me, fair lady!"

She giggled. He grinned. My job was done! I wished them both a good day and turned toward the museum across the cobblestoned walkway.

Tilly Morgenstern was standing in front of the bottom step with Leo behind her.

Was this what Madame Lucinda was warning me about?

I could hear the musicians in the tower above the Main Gate beginning to play. Dancers from the Stage Caravan were beginning to join them. Singers from the Dutchman's Stage were serenading visitors with a funny song. The horsemen were showing off their prowess.

The gate was open, and visitors were streaming in for their day at the Renaissance. There wasn't time to argue with Tilly Morgenstern and her zombie. The museum was still closed, no sign of Manny or Bill.

I took a deep breath and confronted her.

Her cold eyes raked over me. "Where is your shoemaker today, Lady?"

"He should be on his way."

She nodded. "Good. I'll wait. I've heard tell of his elf magic. I want to see it for myself."

"Unless it involves him making boots for you, you'll have to get in line."

"I'm fine with him making boots for me." She grinned. "Not that you could stop me if I wasn't."

"I wouldn't try to stop you. That's why we have security."

People from the gate were lining up behind me. Out of the corner of my eye, I saw Manny, urging Bill to hurry along the cobblestones. There were too many visitors and residents to worry about Tilly's threats. My hand clenched on the cell phone in my pocket anyway.

"Security." Tilly spit on the stairs. Leo did the same.

There were enough residents out to worry about the constant threat of a spitting contest. I cringed when I thought of how that would affect our visitors, but it couldn't be stopped. The tradition of everyone spitting when one person started was too deeply ingrained.

I heard some of Robin Hood's Merry Men pick it up from Tilly. They spat, grinned, and passed it on. Jack Spratt and his wife followed, and then a few monks added their saliva.

Visitors who were waiting to get into the museum liked the idea too and began spitting on the cobblestones behind me. I hoped it would be over before anyone got inside and started spitting on the museum floor.

I didn't indulge, hoping to quell the rising tide. I knew Manny wouldn't spit either, and Bill didn't know about the custom yet. There were unicycle riders spitting from great height on the cobblestones as they went by. A lady in a fancy lemon yellow gown screamed when a pirate spit on the edge of it.

Tilly smiled slyly, no doubt enjoying what she'd started.

Manny finally reached me with Bill. "Let's get inside before this gets out of hand," he urged with a careful eye on Tilly and Leo.

Bill was awake and dressed, but that was all I could say for him. He was still heavy-eyed and walking around in a stupor. He reminded me of Leo.

"I'll need you to move away from the stairs, my good woman." Manny took out his key and nodded at Tilly.

"In a moment." She stepped toward Bill and took his chin in one hand, staring deeply into his bloodshot eyes. A moment later she laughed her sweet little girl laugh. "This shoemaker has no magic. I should flay him where he stands for lying."

Of course, the visitors loved it, thinking it was part of the Village drama performed for their benefit. They applauded Tilly's threat. No doubt many of them knew about Bill and his elf magic from watching the news on TV about Isabelle's death.

I knew Manny was afraid of Tilly and Leo, like everyone

else. He was acting on my behalf so I wouldn't have to deal with her. He knew about our past confrontations.

I loved him for it, but I was the museum director. I had to step up.

"Perhaps later, Tilly Morgenstern. Right now, we are going into the museum for my cobbler to make magic boots and sandals for our visitors." I turned and faced the growing crowd of eager shoppers. I wanted to remind everyone that this was all for show. "You should go back to the Lady in the Lake Tavern, Tilly, and leave us alone."

Tilly knew what I was doing. I hoped she wasn't so far gone that she'd push past the bounds of propriety in front of our visitors.

She nodded and smiled. "Indeed, I shall take this up with you at a later date, Lady Jessie. For now, farewell!"

There was a swirl of red smoke that made everyone cough. The smell of sulfur filled the morning air.

Tilly and Leo were both gone. Visitors applauded, enjoying what they thought was the show. I didn't plan to enlighten them on the reality of what had just happened. I didn't even want to think about it.

My nerves were jangled as I opened the doors to the museum and waved everyone inside. I tried not to let it show. It would be good for publicity. People would tell their friends and relatives what a great show they'd seen.

"What was that?" Manny whispered urgently as we held the doors open for our visitors to enter. "Was it what I thought it was?"

"It is Renaissance Faire Village, good sir." I plastered a pleasant smile on my face and kept it there. "Work with me. Let's get Bill going."

Getting Bill to his cutting table was a major operation. I sent Manny for coffee from the Monastery Bakery. Bill was acting like a large, confused slug. He had a hard time figuring out what he'd been working on the day before. He looked at his boot-making materials as though he'd never seen them.

"I'm not feeling so good, Jessie," he confessed to me and the dozen or so visitors who were gathered around his table. "I think I should lie down for a while."

"Sir Manny has gone for coffee and breakfast at the Monastery Bakery for you." It was good PR to get information in about other spots in the Village. "As soon as you eat one of their delicious cinnamon rolls, you'll feel much better."

Bill nodded, and at least tried to make a go of his craft. He carefully examined a large piece of soft gray leather and set a boot guide on it to cut.

"I'd like a pair of boots made from that." An older woman was wearing a bright gold snood and girdle. "May I be first? I have Lady Visa with me."

"Of course." I smiled at her. "We are selling Master Warren's boots and sandals here until his shop, Bewitching Boots, opens tomorrow."

The visitors murmured happily among each other. They were eager to lay down their Lady Visas and Sir Mastercards on the cutting table. They talked about the magic footwear that they'd heard about. Everyone in the crowded room wanted something made with Bill's elf magic.

Bill couldn't make all the orders we received in a day. He could do a few as the crowds went in and out of the museum. The rest would have to be shipped or picked up later by the visitor.

I took everyone's money or credit and filled out receipts for them. Manny finally got back with a large black coffee and a cinnamon roll for Bill.

"Make a line over here for purchasing the shoemaker's wares." He adjusted the crowd so there was room to watch Bill work. I continued taking payment for at least two dozen pairs of boots, trying to distract everyone while Bill had a chance to eat and caffeinate.

Still the eager faces watched him closely as he sipped coffee and nibbled on the cinnamon roll. Phone cameras captured the not-so-magical moments as Bill nodded off while he was eating. His head fell forward to his worktable.

"What now?" Manny's voice held the edge of panic. "He either has the worst hangover in the world—"

"—or he's being affected by his lack of magic," I whispered. "I've seen him drunk and sleepless in the last few weeks, but not without charm, which he seems to be now."

"No magic?" Manny murmured. "I thought we didn't believe he had magic to begin with."

I told him a hurried sentence or two about what had transpired in Madame Lucinda's tent yesterday.

"So you believe—?"

"I don't know what to believe. We might have to close for a while until he recovers."

A public relations tour guide for the Village fought her way through the crowd on the stairs to bring two reporters in with her. She smiled and shook my hand, blasts of camera flash blinding me. She ignored Manny and went right for Bill. Before I could stop her, the reporters had full access to my barely conscious shoemaker.

"Think fast," Manny suggested.

I graciously descended on the group with my full power as museum director. "Could we do this another time?"

The PR woman in the light gray business suit turned to me with a nervous tick in her pretty smile. "Are you sure? He seems fine to me."

Bill groaned, turned his head, and vomited on her very chic gray and white six-inch heels.

"Yes," I said. "I'm very sure."

Chapter Sixteen

It became a big deal. I had Manny take Bill home and closed the museum so I could accompany the PR woman to the castle. King Harold and Queen Olivia were concerned that Bill was giving the Village a bad reputation.

It was all I could do not to laugh. Bad reputation? Why did they let Tilly and Leo stay in the Village? Why did they allow Gus, the Master at Arms, to pinch every woman who walked into the castle?

I didn't say either of those things. Merlin was also present in the throne room as I arrived. He was still dressed as a wizard with his pointy hat. I knew he only donned a suit and tie if it was really serious. Bill was safe as long as I was careful what I said.

Chase joined us too. I glanced at him. He shrugged.

The throne room was new to the castle. The king and queen (or Harry and Livy as we thought of them in the Village) had added the lavishly appointed area to make the tour of the castle lengthier. There was an extra charge to tour the areas where the king and queen lived. A few visitors had complained that the tour was too short for the money.

The king and queen added the throne room so that visitors could see them dispensing justice and awarding boons to the residents of the Village. It was all for show, of course, like Vegetable Justice that Chase presided over—but without the squishy vegetables or the stocks.

Each morning a group of residents was chosen to either ask for a favor from the royals or plead for mercy for some unknown offense. Adding this feature several times a day had been popular, so much so that they were able to raise the price of the castle tour.

The queen's ladies were dressed in beautifully colored gowns and elaborate headdresses. Princess Pea was present in her cradle with her nanny. Dozens of jugglers, fools, and musicians were around for entertainment. The king's gentlemen flanked him on the royal dais with gorgeous swords. The thrones were actually replicas of thrones from around the world—except executed in wood and painted gold.

I had to admit that the room was impressive.

I curtsied to the king and queen. "I understand that you're upset about the shoemaker's difficulties in the Village, Your Majesties. I can assure you that he will settle in. There has been an unfortunate turn of events that has made his time here difficult."

Sir Reginald (Katharina's father) brought down his staff on the stone floor. "Silence, Lady Jessie! King Harold and Queen Olivia wish to hear a report from the Bailiff before passing judgment on the shoemaker."

"What kind of report?" I questioned angrily. They shut down the museum for this?

"I ask the questions here, Lady." Sir Reginald was at his haughty best.

"That's fine. Ask the questions. I turned away hundreds of people from the museum to be here."

"We understand that the shoemaker was drunk on duty

this morning, Lady Jessie." King Harold finally said. "We are concerned about spending money to get his shop and apartment set-up—at your behest. He has only been here a short time, and yet has been accused of murder, declared himself a user of elf magic, and now is unable to perform his duties."

"There is also the matter of Renaissance Faire Village providing a lavish program to introduce him," Queen Olivia declared. "Explain to us what sort of man you have brought here."

"My dear," the King addressed the Queen. "We should hear her explanation for the shop first. That was more expensive."

"I think my question is a fair one, my liege," Queen Olivia retorted.

Sir Reginald brought down his staff again. "We must first hear from the Bailiff."

The King and Queen glared at him.

He cleared his throat and bowed slightly. "Whatever Your Majesties desire, of course."

I glanced at Chase. "It looks like you're up."

He stepped forward, making an elegant bow to the royals. "My Queen, King Harold—I have been investigating further into the death of Princess Isabelle this very morning. Bill Warren, the new shoemaker, has been cleared of all charges against him in this matter. The police have Sir Dwayne Barker in custody and are questioning him in regard to both the princess's death, and the attack on Rita Martinez from the castle kitchen."

"Do we know the outcome of those questions so far, Sir Bailiff?" the king asked.

"No, Your Highness," Chase replied. "We do not as yet know those answers. I hope to have something more to report later today."

"What about the charges against the shoemaker?" King Harold demanded. "Has he indeed used elf magic in my kingdom?"

"If I may, Your Majesty." Merlin stepped forward. "I have examined the claims of elf magic which the shoemaker suggested. I can tell you that there are no facts to substantiate those claims."

"Thank you, my trusty wizard." The king smiled at him.

"Bill wasn't drunk today either, Your Majesty," I continued, uninvited. Sir Reginald shook his head. I ignored him. "He was ill from something he ate last night. His work is beyond reproach. I shall be happy to show you our sales reports for the past two days."

The King and Queen nodded to one another.

"So we can expect great things from the shoemaker at his new abode?" King Harold raised a royal brow in my direction.

"Absolutely. Sometimes it's difficult for people to settle in, as you well know, but I believe the shoemaker is a fine fit for the Village."

"That is good enough for me, Lady Jessie." Queen Olivia smiled. "You have our thanks for adding to our family here at the Village and increasing our coffers."

It was bogus. The whole thing was a play so that the royals could practice dispensing justice. I'd shut down the museum for nothing. It would be hard to get that crowd back today.

Maybe it was okay since Bill wasn't feeling well. I curtsied to the king and queen and left the throne room. Chase followed quickly after me.

"What happened with Bill?" he asked.

I shrugged. "He's sick. I hope he'll be better tomorrow." I didn't mention that the shoemaker had been up drinking half the night. "What about Sir Dwayne? Did anyone see him come into the castle last night?"

"I haven't talked to anyone who saw him, but you know how it is here. There are too many people living in the castle for anyone to notice who goes in and out."

"What about Gus? He wasn't at the gate the day Isabelle died, you know. I've been thinking about it since then.

What's up with him?"

"He's having an affair with one of the new women at The King's Tarts. That's all. He usually confines his dalliances to someone in the castle. He's been roaming a little further than usual."

"Maybe there needs to be someone at the gate to relieve him," I suggested. "What now?"

"I don't know. I'll keep trying to find someone who saw Sir Dwayne come in last night. We don't have a time for him, but neither do the police. Although they have plenty to charge him with after this morning."

"Excuse me, good sir." The woman was one of Isabelle's ladies. I remembered her from the museum and the garden. "I overheard your problem. I can tell you what time Sir Dwayne came into the castle last night."

Chase smiled at her. "Did you see him come in? You're Victoria, right?"

"Yes, sir." She dipped into a tiny curtsy. "I was going through Princess Isabelle's clothing as the king and queen requested. They want to give away what they can of hers. Her suite will be used for Princess Pea in the future."

"And what time did you see Sir Dwayne return?" Chase asked.

"It was before two a.m., sir. I noticed because he came to the princess's room to retrieve some articles of his clothing."

"I see. Thank you, Victoria."

"Sir?" She stopped him from leaving. "I was wondering what happened this morning that made the police arrest Sir Dwayne? Do they believe he attacked Rita?"

"I don't know yet," Chase said. "Sir Dwayne held Lady Jessie hostage and tried to flee the Village. The gun he was holding went off, and he was injured. It doesn't look good for him."

Victoria's face paled, and she put her hand to her throat. "You mean he is going to die?"

"No. He'll be fine, but the charges are serious against him even without Rita's attack."

I was surprised at Chase being so frank with the woman. Usually he was a little cagier about his answers regarding an investigation. When Victoria curtsied and left us, I asked him about it.

"I figure she's been through enough with Isabelle's death. I didn't want to jerk her around about it. You know how tight everyone is here at the castle."

I couldn't disagree with his reasoning. I wondered if Victoria might be smitten with Sir Dwayne—as everyone else seemed to be. It seemed odd that she hadn't asked about the investigation into Princess Isabelle's death.

I went to check on Bill. He was still sleeping it off. Chase and I agreed that we'd take our lunch breaks together and visit Rita at the hospital. I went back to the Dungeon to change out of my Village clothes and into jeans and a tank top. I grabbed some clothes for Chase and went to meet him at Peter's Pub where we'd be closer to the Main Gate.

We didn't eat at Peter's though. As soon as Chase had changed clothes, we left the Village and stopped at our favorite burger place from the 'outside' world.

"Now if you really want to do something good for the Village," he said. "You'd talk the king and queen into having a cheeseburger place."

I laughed. "The queen likes you better. Maybe you can talk her into it."

"Methinks the Village will never have a cheeseburger heaven along the cobblestones. We'll have to sneak out occasionally in our street clothes to eat such as this." He took a big bite of his burger and washed it down with soda.

"Probably just as well." I sipped some of my chocolate shake. "We don't need the fat and cholesterol."

"I think the story Victoria told us at the castle is going to stick, Jessie. I talked to a few other members of Isabelle's retinue who saw Dwayne come in at the same time last night. I called Detective Almond. They probably won't hold him— unless we press charges against him."

I munched a few fries. "What do you think?"

He shrugged. "I think they should lock him up and throw away the key. He was holding a gun on both of us. He could have hurt you."

"But he shot himself. Maybe that atones for it."

"I don't think so. If I wouldn't have shown up, no telling where you'd be right now. Maybe he didn't plan to hurt you, but he had a gun. I think he deserves whatever he gets."

"That's the police training talking," I argued. "Sir Dwayne was desperate. I kind of blame myself because I told the police I'd seen him with Rita. That didn't make him guilty of anything."

Chase pointed at me with a French fry. "If we don't press charges against him, he'll walk, and what happens next time he gets desperate? I'm going to tell Detective Almond that I want to charge him. I guess it's up to you if you don't."

I couldn't believe he could be so one-sided about it. I could clearly see Sir Dwayne's position. "Maybe it's because you've never had someone suspect you of something you didn't do. It makes you desperate, and you do stupid things."

"So you won't back me up on this? It's going to look lame if one of us presses charges and the other one doesn't."

"I'm sorry. I know what he did was wrong, but if he isn't guilty of hurting Rita . . ."

"We don't know about Isabelle yet," he reminded me.

"That's the way I feel." I knew I was being stubborn about it, but I didn't want to see Sir Dwayne go to jail if he didn't really hurt anyone.

"Okay. If that's the way you feel."

We finished eating in silence, and then Chase drove to the hospital.

Rita was in good spirits, despite her bruises and cuts. She was sitting up against several pillows, holding court for her friends more regally than Queen Olivia in her throne room.

When she saw us, her eyes narrowed. "Chase, if you're here to question me about what happened, you might as well go. I don't remember anything. Whoever it was attacked me did it from behind with something hard, like a baseball bat. After that first hit in the head, I didn't know anything until I woke up here."

Chase leaned over her and carefully kissed her cheek. "I'm not here to ask questions. How are you feeling?"

I put our balloons that we'd brought from the hospital gift shop on the table beside her.

"I'm sorry." Rita wiped a tear away. "The police have asked me so many questions. I just want to go home. No telling what's happening in my kitchen. I'll be hearing about it for weeks."

There were several knaves, a few varlets, and three or four madmen there with her. Two of the serving wenches from the castle were also present. Everyone tried to keep the conversation upbeat. Mostly we talked about which of the new actors would make the cut. Everyone had their favorite.

"I heard Sir Dwayne was arrested." Rita shrugged off the lightweight discussion. "Do they think he killed Isabelle?"

"I don't know," Chase admitted. "He pulled a gun on me and Jessie. I think he could be capable of killing Isabelle."

Rita started crying. "He's not like that. You have to talk to the police for him. They'll listen to you."

Chase glanced at me. I grinned back and stuck out my tongue.

"We'll have to see how the investigation goes," he said. "Everything is up in the air right now. We should know something more later today or tomorrow. Sir Dwayne was trying to get out of the Village, Rita. He wasn't acting like an innocent man."

"All right," she said softly. "I know you'll do the best you can to help him, Chase. Thank you."

It was only a few minutes later that a nurse came and shooed us all out of Rita's hospital room. It was fun walking down the hall with the costumed knaves, varlets, and others. Everyone stared and whispered. Kids laughed and pointed.

Chase and I didn't fit in with the group, but that was only on the outside. We were all part of the crazy group from the Ren Faire, as I'd heard one woman whisper as we went by.

We said goodbye at the outside door after Chase had offered everyone else a ride back to the Village. The group was out on their day off, and headed for the beach.

"Don't say it." Chase took out his car keys. "What is it with Sir Dwayne that you and Rita want to defend him?"

"Well, Rita's in love with him. I'm just not willing to put him in prison for what happened today."

As we walked into the parking deck, Chase put his arms around me and held me close. "That could have been you that was shot today, Jessie. I can't even think about it. I wish I'd had the chance to kick Sir Dwayne around some this morning before the police got there. Do you understand that?"

"I do." I slid my fingers through his hair. "I love you too. I was worried about you when you came out of the apartment. I was hoping he and I would get out without you seeing us. I wanted to protect you."

He kissed me. "I love you for that, but next time I'll do what my gut tells me and take care of the problem myself."

"Don't even say that," I urged him. "You're not a real police officer. You just play one in the Village. You're a lawyer and a horse lover. You like to twirl spaghetti on your fork. If this starts taking you over, we'll leave the Village— or at least become craft people. I won't let you become like Detective Almond."

"Okay." He hugged me close, finally seeming to understand my distress. "I don't see that happening, but we'll do it your way—at least for now. I love you."

"I love you too, Sir Bailiff. But I would love you as much if you carved wooden horses too."

We finished the walk to our car with our arms around each other. I hoped I was right about not pressing charges against Sir Dwayne. I hoped I wouldn't be sorry later.

Chapter Seventeen

When we got back to the Village, we changed clothes and went our separate ways. Chase had several calls from his security people. I wanted to check on Bill again.

There was a huge afternoon crowd on the cobblestones. The line for hatchet throwing near the bakery had to be directed away from the Main Gate so more visitors could get in. It was the same everywhere, with long lines of visitors waiting for the next act at the Dutchman's Stage as well as Stage Caravan.

I checked at the tiny house that Fred and Bill had been sharing. Neither one of them were there. On a hunch, I walked toward the new shop that was all but ready for Bill's amazing talents. The big blue/green sign that read Bewitching Boots glittered in the sunlight.

I saw Bill through the window. He was seated at his big worktable. I went inside and looked around. The construction crew had done a great job on the downstairs shop area. I hoped the upstairs living space was as good. Hundreds of pairs of boots hung on the walls, and sandals filled space on the shelves.

"Are you feeling better?" I asked him.

"Thanks, Jessie. I am." He smiled, but there was something missing from his usual happy spirit. "I've been sitting here looking at my leather and patterns. I can't figure out what to do with them. It's all left me now. I think the elf magic was the only thing that made me a cobbler. Without it, I'm nothing."

I sat at the table with him. "I'm sure it will be fine once you feel better." I didn't want to encourage his belief that elf magic was all that was important about him—especially since I'd convinced the Village to build this shop and apartment.

"Look." He took off the red cap he wore. "I can't even wiggle my ears anymore. My hands are shaking. I don't know how to read my own patterns. I'm sorry I've let you down."

"Don't worry about me. Take some time to get yourself together. Maybe if you play around with your patterns and materials, it will all come back to you."

If not, we'll go visit Madame Lucinda again and get your elf magic back.

He still had time to recover before we took that drastic step, but I needed my cobbler back again. If it meant he had to restore his magic, so be it.

With nothing much to do since the museum was closed, I wandered up to the Field of Honor to watch the next joust.

The bleachers were packed with visitors. Each side of the field had their own cheerleader who was explaining how the scoring worked and who the visitors should cheer for. I was standing on the side designated for the King's Champion. The other side of the field would shout for the Black Knight.

I saw Chase near the royal grandstand as I watched the king's procession of jugglers, fools, and gentlemen ascend the stairs so they could look down on the proceedings from their box high above the field. I tried to catch Chase's eye, but he was already moving away. It looked as though some of his new knights would joust that day.

Wanting a better view, and a chance to hang around with my husband, I skirted around the edge of the fence as both sides of the field were practicing their cheers. Something was wrong. I didn't see the Black Knight, or any of his followers, on the field or behind the grandstand. Usually this was a bigger group than the king or queen's retinues. The Black Knight was more popular than whoever jousted for the royals.

"What's up?" I asked Chase when I'd finally reached him.

"It looks like Charlie isn't going to make the joust. He was pulled over for speeding on Highway 17. They're arresting him for going over a hundred."

"On the main road going through Myrtle Beach?" I shook my head. "How is that even possible? Traffic is always bumper to bumper through there."

"I don't know—but you know him. If there's a way to do something dangerous, he'll find it."

"Are they cancelling the joust?"

"No. Too many visitors." He started walking toward the stables and the knights' dressing area.

"You? You're going to be the Black Knight? You haven't seriously jousted in forever. You might get hurt."

"Thanks for the vote of confidence." He grinned. "If it makes you feel any better, I'm jousting against all the newbies I've been training. Maybe I can manage to stay on my horse, ancient rider that I am."

I followed him into the Black Knight's dressing room. It was clearly marked with a huge black star on the door. "That's not what I meant. I'm sure you can still joust. You do it every day in training. But on the field is different."

"I'll try to take that into account, milady. Thank you. I have to get dressed now."

"Let me help you. I'll be your squire. I'm sure none of

Charlie's squires are around. I know how to do this."

"Okay." He shrugged as he removed his leather vest and loose-fitting shirt. "Fetch me my undergarments, wench."

I found the white T-shirts the jousters wore under their armor. Charlie and Chase were about the same size. I also found the britches Charlie wore, but Chase decided to wear what he had.

The armor worn by the knights in the Village wasn't as heavy as what the real knights wore during the Middle Ages. It was really made more to be attractive than protective. The Black Knight's armor was black (not surprising), and very shiny. His squire did a good job taking care of it.

Mostly the knights who jousted only wore the headpiece and breastplate as tokens of who they were. The helm had a visor and an elaborate comb on the top that included black and red feathers. Chase also wore the gorget neckpiece above the breastplate. He decided against the pauldrons that were the protective shoulder pieces, but wore the gauntlets.

"What about the plackart?" I asked about the midsection piece below the breastplate.

"No. It's too hot for that." He pulled up the hood that he'd wear under the headpiece.

"If you take a hit lower than the breastplate, you'll be sorry."

"You're kind of bossy for a squire." He smiled at me, and gave me a quick kiss. "If my new recruits can hit any part of me, they'll be lucky."

"If you don't have any faith in them why are you letting them joust so soon?"

"Because they need the experience."

He had me pin on the black cape that accentuated his identity. I offered to get his lances. Are you using a sword?"

"Not really, but I'd like the scabbard for show." He wiped the sweat from his forehead. "It's too hot for jousting in the afternoon."

"You should mention that at the next meeting in the royal throne room." I grabbed the three lances that flew his black standard.

"Yeah, like they'd care." He stood back and held his arms out at his sides. "How do I look? Sufficiently evil, I hope."

"You're the devil," I said with a grin. "Is Katharina jousting today?"

"Yeah. I'm keeping her identity a secret until the joust is over. Then she can pull off her helmet and let all that red hair fly."

"What about Foxfire?"

"Too sick to participate, although he's doing better since the vet saw him. That's another problem. She isn't used to the horse she's riding. I'm going to have to fall on the ground to let my new jousters take me off my horse."

I planted a big kiss on his lips. "Just don't get too full of yourself, sir. You can be hurt just like anyone else."

"I get it. Now fetch my horse, squire."

The Black Knight always rode a large black stallion. The horses were supplied by the Templar Knights who were the best trainers I'd ever seen. They could get horses to do things I didn't know horses could do. I knew in that way that Chase at least had a great advantage.

I found his horse in the stables wearing his colors, and tugged at the bridle to get him to follow me. The horse snorted a few times, but eventually we got back to the dressing area. I put the block near the elaborate saddle so Chase could mount in the stiff armor.

"Good luck," I said when he was in the saddle.

"Thanks. Love you. You have to be the prettiest squire ever." He winked, and the horse trotted away.

I could hear the announcements that preceded the joust. They were being made by the king and members of his retinue over the loud speaker. There was no way they could be heard above the crowd without it, even though it was technically a breach of Renaissance rules.

Chase rode out on the field as I took the lances to his starting point. I wasn't exactly dressed as a squire. People were sure to point that out to me later. It was an emergency. Everyone would have to suck it up.

Even more people were in the bleachers now, and a large group of residents was standing at the fence. No doubt, word of Chase jousting had reached along the cobblestones and everyone was curious.

After Chase and his horse had been cheered by his side, and booed by the other side, the opposing jousters came on the field. Again the cheerleaders led the jeers and cheers according to their spots. There were far more Huzzahs! than boos. One of the cheerleaders wasn't doing a very good job.

Chase would be jousting against one of the three knights—whoever the champion was of their contests. One of them was having a rough time with a large chestnut mare. I suspected it was Katharina, although it was impossible to tell by their unmarked armor and similar britches. Their helmets kept their faces and identities secret.

As the first two knights began to joust, Chase removed his visor and began making outrageous, completely obnoxious remarks, goading the knights and the other side of the field. That was part of his job as the Black Knight.

In the Queen's Joust, her champion—the handsome and charismatic Sir Marcus Bishop—would remark on the beauty of his hair and the radiance of his shield and armor. His challengers never won. They were regularly knocked off their horses to uproarious laughter.

The Black Knight was evil, even though he still had his own cheering section. I laughed at Chase's handsome face as he jeered the competing knights who wanted to fight him. The very idea that his face could be evil was hilarious to me. I've seen him angry and stern when he was working as the Bailiff. But evil? No way.

The knight that I believed was Katharina triumphed over her opponent as she sent him to the ground with a fine blow to the chest from her lance. The crowd went wild, stomping their feet and yelling Huzzah! The next opponent got ready for the contest.

The second knight was tougher. He lasted for a few rounds. Katharina again tilted her lance into his chest, and he lost his seat on his horse. I was sure it was her by then. She had a riding style all her own even though she wasn't on her Foxfire. She was going to make an excellent jouster. I wouldn't be surprised to see her riding as the king or queen's champion at some point. She had grace and strength that everyone watching recognized.

"Are you ready?" I asked Chase as I handed him first lance. "She's aiming for below the breastplate. You should've worn the plackart."

"I'll avoid that area, squire. Thank you for your good advice."

It was part of the act that the Black Knight was even mean to his faithful squire. I knew what to expect as I turned away. I felt Chase's boot at the back of my skirt and fell face first into a pile of hay.

That really riled up the spectators on the opposite side of the field. The cheerleader on Chase's side led her group in loud guffaws. I got to my feet and shook my fist at my master. Everyone loved it. I hadn't forgotten the old routine.

Chase and Katharina squared off against each other on opposite ends of the field. The Black Knight was never allowed to accept a favor for his joust. The challenger always received a favor from the cheerleader on that side of the field.

Katharina held her horse in check as the cheerleader gave her a red rose. Loud Huzzahs! followed. But she didn't return to her spot where she would face Chase. Instead, she quietly moved her horse to where I was standing. She handed me the rose she'd just received.

"I joust for you, my lady." Her voice was muffled but understandable from behind her visor.

No one knew what to do. Chase's spectators yelled Huzzah! and so did Katharina's. I smiled and curtsied to her. She was definitely one of a kind.

Her horse went back to its starting position, and she raised her lance. Chase lowered his visor and assumed the correct position with his lance. The sultry day grew quiet around us. The king dropped the pennant, and the joust began.

Normally, the Black Knight always prevailed against his opponent. But I knew Chase had something else in mind since he'd described Katharina removing her helmet while still on her horse. That meant he meant to lose.

One of the first things he taught perspective jousters was how to fall from the horse without getting hurt. I knew he'd make it good for the sake of the drama. I held my breath as she came toward him, her lance ready to unseat him.

Chase moved slightly to the right as she bore down on him. Her lance missed him completely. The momentum of missing her target almost knocked Katharina to the hay-covered ground. She held up her hand, signaling that she was all right, and the pair got ready for the next joust.

As I thought, Chase hit his target in the next joust. Katharina clung to her horse despite the hard blow to her chest. She'd worn her plackart. It protected her from his lance, but not from the strong push that might have unseated her.

Again, she held up her hand to show that she was all right. There were loud Huzzahs! and plenty of foot stomping from both sides of the field. The riders got back in position again for the last joust.

I watched with as much excitement as the people around me. More residents had lined up to see the finale. I wondered what their response would be to see Chase fall from his horse, and Katharina unmasked as the first female jouster. It would be a moment everyone would remember and discuss for a long time.

The horses started toward each other again. They snorted, and their hooves threw up clods of sand and hay behind them. The lances aimed true and straight at their opponents. Music usually played from the grandstand during the joust, but even the musicians were silent, watching the event.

The lances met, their tips moving past each other until they hit their targets. Chase sent his lance to the left just slightly to avoid hitting Katharina. She, however, kept her aim where it was supposed to be. Her lance hit Chase below his breastplate, knocking him from his horse.

Both sides of the field started shouting as Katharina took a winning lap around the inside of the fence. Chase's cheerleader finally got her people under control and they began to boo.

I could see the stunned faces on the residents around me. If Chase had ever been unseated from his horse, it was a long time ago. This wasn't what they'd come to see.

Then Katharina's big moment was at hand. She doffed her helmet, and the sun glinted on her glorious long hair. There was no doubt at that moment that the knight was a woman—even though some of the knights also sported longish hair. She raised her lance high, and the crowd went wild.

I ran to where Chase had fallen, concerned that he hadn't gotten up yet. His horse stood above him trying to eat the grass at the side of the fence. I removed his helmet. "Are you okay?"

Chapter Eighteen

"Just got the wind knocked out of me," he wheezed, barely able to speak. I examined his abdominal muscles beneath his T-shirt. The area was slightly red but no damage done. "Next time you say plackart, I'll say yes ma'am."

I threw myself on top of him. "You're okay. She's really good. No one can believe she beat you."

He lay back against the sand. "We all have to lose sometime."

"But you lost on purpose. I knew that's what you were going to do."

"Yeah, well, let's not talk about it right now. I think I'm getting too old to fall off a horse."

The joust was over. The bewildered King Harold was giving the victor's purse—fake gold coins that had to be returned—to Katharina.

D'Amos, Daisy, and Phil Ferguson from the Sword Spotte, ducked under the fence to find out what had happened. I moved back to grasp the horse's reins.

"Are you okay?" Daisy ran her hand up and down Chase's chest.

"Daisy!" I called her off before it got embarrassing.

Her round face turned bright red, and she pulled her hand back. "Simmer down. I was just feeling for broken ribs."

"Let us help you to your feet," D'Amos said. With Phil's help, they got Chase off the ground.

"Thanks, guys." He removed his helmet, and I helped him take off his breastplate. He'd dropped one of his gauntlets, and I went to get it.

"What in the world happened to you, big guy?" My brother, Tony, asked.

Good news! He wasn't wearing a monk's robe.

"It was staged, of course," Sam DaVinci said as he joined the fast-growing crowd of residents. "Anyone could see that."

"You did a bang up job, my boy," Merlin told him. "And who is that lovely vision in armor?"

"Our newest knight and jouster, Katharina," Chase said. "She's something, isn't she?"

Diego and Lorenzo, the Tornado twins, paraded their little pig around on her leash. "I want someone to tell me why the lady knight gave Jessie her favor. There must be a punchline."

"She was just saying thank you," I explained.

"Yes!" Lorenzo galloped around behind the pig. "I would like very much for her to say thank you to me."

I grabbed Tony's arm and pulled him away from the group. "No robe?"

"No robe. I couldn't bake bread without burning it. I don't know how they do it."

"What now?" I was so glad for him and the Brotherhood that he hadn't become a monk.

Tony nodded toward D'Amos. "I'm working with animals. They needed someone."

"Maybe that's your calling." I smiled at him, wishing I

understood him better. I kept waiting for him to grow up. It never seemed to happen.

Katharina rode her horse toward us. She smiled at Chase. "I think they like me. The king asked me to be his champion."

"Great." Chase was still brushing sand and hay from his clothes. "Just don't accept any personal invitations to the castle from him."

Daisy agreed. "Yeah, Harry has been a model husband since Pea was born. I wouldn't count on that continuing."

Merlin set his pointed hat straight on his head. "And you don't want to make an enemy of Livy. She takes things very personally."

Katharina paid attention to everyone's advice as Diego and Lorenzo kept trying to get her to look at them. Her eyes, it seemed, were only for Tony. "Are you ready?"

Tony winked at me and jumped on the horse behind Katharina. "I'm always ready."

As they rode away together, Diego was hurt. "What does he have besides a handsome face and a firm tush? Why didn't she take me?"

Lorenzo hugged his brother. "Cheer up. You always have me."

Diego pushed him away. "I believe that is part of the problem, sir. Please take your pig, and leave me at once. I am grieving for the jouster who might have skewered me."

***

I didn't mind that it wasn't only my talk with Tony that had kept him out of the Brotherhood of the Sheaf. Maybe he and Katharina would work out. I'd always thought the right woman could be a blessing for my brother. He had to quit hanging out with the fairies and the other Village women who weren't serious about a relationship.

I cleaned Chase's armor back at the changing area while he showered. I was glad that Katharina and I could be friends, especially if she was going to date Tony. I also didn't need more people like Tilly in the Village, who wanted my head on a platter.

On that note, Wanda appeared. "I thought Chase was a goner for a moment." She traced one finger down the edge of his breastplate, not quite touching it, and yet sparks followed her finger on the metal. "Too bad. He and I could have made lovely spectral music together."

"You mean like you did in real life, right?" It was a snarky thing to say, but Chase had never liked Wanda.

"You don't know everything that went on here while you were teaching at school. There were all those long winter nights when Chase was alone."

"I have a pretty good idea." I continued rubbing the cleaning solution on the gauntlets. I wasn't sure if Charlie would be back anytime soon, but I didn't want the next Black Knight to find his armor dirty.

Wanda disappeared for a moment, but before I could take a breath of relief that she was gone, she was back again.

"I didn't know Chase sang in the shower." She grinned like a demon.

"It doesn't count if he can't see you and he doesn't know you're there."

"No, but I can certainly see him in all his glory!"

"Go away. Find someone else to haunt." I was determined not to let her get under my skin.

"Speaking of haunts, I believe Princess Isabelle is haunting the castle garden. I was over there last night and heard her crying."

I put down the gauntlet. "Seriously?"

"It sometimes happens when someone has been murdered. They can't find peace." Wanda rolled her eyes back into her head—a ghastly trick she'd learned. "I know all about it. Maybe I can give her a few pointers to get her going on the right track."

Great! All we need at the Village is another malevolent ghost. "Leave her alone. She'll find her own way."

"The poor thing just wants someone to solve her murder. I suppose she'll have to do without since you and Chase can't seem to figure out who killed her."

"The police have Sir Dwayne in custody."

"As if lover boy killed her. Is that the best you can do?"

"Do you know who killed her?" I realized that a straight answer from her could save us some time. I wasn't sure how I'd know, or trust, that it was accurate but it was worth a shot.

"Perhaps. But I'm not telling you, Jessie. Not unless you give me something in return."

I searched her frightening blue face that I'd somehow grown accustomed to since her death, and wondered what she'd ask for. "Such as?"

"I want greater access." She licked her lips. "I want to be in your apartment again."

I started cleaning the second gauntlet. "Forget it. I'll figure it out on my own. Leave Isabelle alone."

"All right then. I'll tell the princess you aren't interested in catching her killer. Ta-ta."

She vanished an instant before Chase got out of the shower with a towel wrapped around his hips. "Did I hear you talking to someone?"

"Wanda. She was in the shower with you, and claims to know who killed Isabelle. She said she'll tell me if I let her back in our place."

"What? That's just wrong." Chase dried his long hair on a towel. "No way. She's probably lying anyway."

"You're probably right." I looked up at him. "She also said that Isabelle is haunting the castle garden where she died."

"You believe her?"

"I don't know. I guess it wouldn't hurt to check it out. Maybe Isabelle knows who killed her."

He shrugged. "I suppose it's worth a visit. How do you talk to a ghost?"

"If it's like talking to Wanda, the same way you do when they're alive." I looked at the red mark on his abs that was slowly becoming a large bruise. "That looks painful."

"I'm sure I could do with a massage, if you know someone who's willing." He grinned and dropped his towel.

I locked the door.

* * *

We waited in the castle garden after midnight. The Village was quiet by the time we'd walked up the hill. Gus was absent from the castle gate again, and we let ourselves into the back of the structure. The moon was drifting above us in a dreamy, star-filled sky. I could think of many other things I'd rather be doing than waiting for a ghost to appear.

But if Isabelle was haunting the garden—and she knew who killed her—it would be worthwhile.

"I still think we should've brought Madame Lucinda," Chase whispered. "She seems to have experience in this kind of thing."

"I have experience with a ghost too. And I don't want to involve Madame Lucinda if we don't have to." I glanced around the dark garden that surrounded us. The smell of roses perfumed the night air while cicadas and frogs serenaded us.

Chase didn't realize how scary Madame Lucinda was. He couldn't see her dragon or anything else magical in her tent. He also didn't know that she'd taken Bill's elf magic. There was too much going on between me and her to casually invite her to a ghost hunt. I had a feeling that my debt to her might end up having to be repaid by something I didn't want to do. It was just an uncomfortable feeling I had when I was with her, as though she was waiting to ask a favor of me.

If we couldn't find Isabelle's ghost out here—I might have to reconsider.

I knew Isabelle wouldn't want me around. We had bad blood between us, even more than me and Wanda. Chase wouldn't be able to see or hear her since he couldn't see or hear Wanda. Madame Lucinda might be a good intermediary.

"Why don't you like her?" he asked. "She's always very

pleasant to me."

"I like her. She's nice. I can't really explain any more than that. I'll call her if we need to. First, I want to make sure Wanda wasn't lying."

Chase leaned back against the bench where we were sitting. "I wish she'd go ahead and appear. I have an early morning meeting with the new man who's in charge of the Templar Knights."

"Yeah? What's he like?"

"Young. Very young. He says he's eighteen, but I think he may only be fourteen or fifteen, tops."

"That's young. How did he get to be in charge?"

"He's the best rider I've ever seen. The men respect that. They don't care if he's too young to drink in the pub."

"Are you going to let him lead the horsemen?"

"I don't think I have much choice."

I heard a terrible sound in the brush around us. "Did you hear something?" I whispered.

"Yes." Chase sat up. "Is that Isabelle?"

There was whispering and then moaning again. I wasn't sure if it was a cat or someone crying. I didn't think there were any cats living in the castle, although I wasn't completely sure. I knew the queen had a small Yorkie. Maybe she had a cat too.

Chase got to his feet. "Isabelle? Is that you?"

The wailing continued. It seemed to get closer to the courtyard. I stood beside Chase. My heart was pounding. It was difficult to breathe.

"Isabelle?" I called into the darkness as well. "If you're here, show yourself."

There was a bright light from above us. I grabbed Chase's hand as I looked up. The light resolved into a gauzy figure. "Look! There she is. Wanda was right."

"Isabelle!" Chase said.

As I continued to watch, there was a loud cry that reverberated through the night. Tears started to my eyes as the bright, female form above us plummeted toward the stones at our feet. For a moment I could see the startled and terrified expression on Isabelle's dying face as she lay there facing the sky.

It was as though I was Isabelle. I felt the terrible pain that raced through her broken body. Her heart slowed as her lungs filled with blood. She/I knew that we would never walk again—never see another day.

I felt a woman's skirt touch my arm, and looked up into her face as she stared down at me. I reached for her, begging for help though I couldn't say the words.

My head dropped to the stones with her name on my lips.

"Rita."

Chapter Nineteen

"No! No! No! Rita can't be the killer." I had raged about what I'd seen since I'd awakened on a sofa in the castle.

Chase had brought me here and called an ambulance. I had him cancel that call when I woke up. There was nothing wrong with me—except that I'd seen Isabelle's death as though it was my own.

"Shh! Keep your voice down," he said. "We don't want everyone in the castle to wake up and discuss this with us."

"Sorry." I dropped down on the sofa again, exhausted. "I don't believe Rita killed Isabelle. She's just not like that."

"It was your vision, or whatever. There's no proof that Rita did anything. Let's say that what you saw was real. Rita could've checked on Isabelle. That's why she was close to her."

"You're right." I grasped at the explanation. "That's what it was. It has to be. The last thing Isabelle saw was Rita checking on her after she came out in the garden to smoke. Isabelle didn't die right away."

Chase lounged back in a matching red velvet chair. We were in the visitor's lounge where people waited for audiences with the king and queen. "It wasn't real anyway, Jessie. If you're feeling better, let's go home."

"But why would Isabelle want me to see that moment if it didn't mean anything? She could have showed me the face of the person who pushed her off the terrace."

"We should definitely go home. You have to get a good night's sleep and forget all this."

I stopped pacing and stared at him. "I have to talk to Madame Lucinda. She'll know what this means."

"I thought you didn't want to involve her."

"Not in looking for a ghost who might or might not appear. This is different. I need to see her."

He got to his feet. "Okay. Let's find out if she's still awake."

We left the castle. Gus was at the gate, a big smile on his face. "What ho, night travelers. Where do you go so late? Were you two staying at the castle tonight? I didn't get a memo on that. They're supposed to let me know if anyone unusual is here."

"We're not unusual," Chase said. "And if I find you away from your post again, I'm going to tell the king. There's a reason you're supposed to be here. If you need help, I can have some of my security guys split shifts with you."

Gus wasn't intimidated by Chase's words. "If I need help, I'll ask for it. What are you and Jessie doing here so late?"

"A better question might be—where were you when Isabelle was killed?" I asked. "I walked out this way. You were gone."

"I can't stand here all the time," Gus replied.

"Exactly," Chase added. "This is why you need help—unless you're going to start dating someone in the castle again. These walks into the Village aren't going to work."

"I'll take care of it." Gus's voice was gruff. "You two,

get out of here. I'll see you later."

There was still some activity in the otherwise quiet Village. Lights and sound were coming from the Lady in the Lake Tavern as we went by. I didn't care what was going on there, and hurried Chase past it before he felt the need to knock on Tilly's door.

"I can't believe you're afraid of her," he razzed me. "I've seen you stand up to other people without even thinking about it."

"It's not just her. It's the zombie that's always with her."

"He's not a zombie, Jessie." Chase laughed. "Tilly has her own myth she's trying to perpetrate. Don't fall for it."

"Whatever—just don't pick fights with them. As far as I know, you don't have any white magic to combat her black magic."

He put his arm around me. "Whatever you say."

As we continued around the edge of Mirror Lake, there was music and the sound of incredibly bad singing coming from the Queen's Revenge pirate ship. Grigg, the ex-police officer turned pirate, yelled drunkenly at us. Chase held up one hand and saluted him.

The remainder of the walk to Madame Lucinda's tent was quiet and dark. I couldn't tell as we approached if there were lights on in her tent or not. I didn't want to simply walk in, but it's hard to knock on cloth.

Before I could face this conundrum, the fortuneteller herself came out into the moonlight. "Lady Jessie. Sir Bailiff. A pleasant evening to you."

"You knew we were coming," I said as I nudged Chase.

"Jessie has had a weird night," he said. "I hope we didn't disturb you."

"Not at all." She was as gracious as ever. "I was actually expecting Jessie and the cobbler. I felt sure he'd want his magic back by now."

"He still has some time to reclaim it," I reminded her. "I think you're right. He's miserable without it."

She shrugged. "As is frequently the case. But if you're

not here for that reason, what is the purpose of your visit?"

Chase glanced around. There were a few monks walking the cobblestones with lanterns. They wished us all a good night. "It might be better if we go inside. I don't think Jessie wants to share what she has to say with everyone in the Village."

Madame Lucinda opened the tent flap and stood back. "Please. I am always happy to have guests."

We stepped through the portal and sat at her table that held a crystal ball. I took a quick peek at the shelf above her chair. The dragon was there, asleep.

"Do you see it now?" I whispered to Chase.

He looked up and nodded. "Yes. I've seen it before. A really nice dragon statue. I don't see it moving or breathing fire, do you?"

"No. Not right now."

Madame Lucinda took her place opposite us. "Buttercup is resting. Dragons are not creatures of the night. They love the sun."

Chase glanced up again. The dragon hadn't moved. "Uh–sure."

"Never mind." I concentrated instead on Madame Lucinda. "I've had some kind of vision, or I was able to see through Princess Isabelle's eyes as she died. I know that sounds strange, but that's what it was like."

She sat forward, her eyes deeply focused on me. "What was this vision?"

I explained why we'd been in the garden and what I'd seen. "But I know Rita didn't kill her. Why wouldn't Isabelle want me to see who the killer is?"

"Perhaps she doesn't know. Perhaps you saw what she saw. It was true with Wanda, was it not? She didn't see the face of her killer and couldn't communicate that to you."

"That's true," I agreed. "But this was so much different. I didn't have this kind of experience with Wanda."

"Each experience is different."

"I know Rita. I know she didn't kill Isabelle."

"And she didn't beat herself up," Chase added. "Just because you saw one part of this doesn't mean it was the whole picture, Jessie. Sir Dwayne still looks like our best suspect."

Madame Lucinda shifted her pointed gaze to him. "I believe you are also only allowing yourself to see one part of the picture, Sir Bailiff. You must look at the entire image to find your answers."

"Thank you." I realized our session was over.

"But—" Chase was determined to get answers.

"I am fatigued." Madame Lucinda got to her feet. "Excuse me, Bailiff, Lady Jessie."

Chase stalked out of the purple and gold tent.

I started to follow him, but Madame Lucinda held me back.

"The last sight we have is impressed on the mind's eye," she said. "It could have easily been the ground Isabelle fell upon, or a tree. You must learn why she saw Rita Martinez. Then you will have your answer."

"Thank you." I inclined my head in respect. "There's something to this hoodoo stuff, isn't there?"

"Indeed, Lady Jessie."

I left her and caught up with Chase. He was already to the Monastery Bakery and hadn't noticed I wasn't with him. "Hey! Where's the fire?"

He stopped and glanced around. "Sorry. I thought you were with me."

I ducked under his arm so it was across my shoulders. "Always."

He kissed me. "Let's go home."

* * *

I lay in bed for hours trying to figure out what Madame Lucinda was trying to tell me about Isabelle—and I'd forgotten to tell her about the vision I'd had of her outside the Dungeon.

Maybe she was reinforcing my own feelings that Rita

hadn't killed the princess. Yes, they wanted the same man, but Rita knew as well as I did that Isabelle wouldn't want him for long. All she had to do was wait and catch Sir Dwayne on the rebound.

I had to do much the same thing with Chase. He'd been dating Isabelle when we met, too. It wasn't that long after that we'd met that she and Chase weren't together anymore. I'd never asked if the decision to break up was Chase's or Isabelle's. It wasn't like Chase met me and we fell madly in love. Our romance came about after knowing each other for a while.

The point was that Rita might have been jealous, but I didn't believe she would've killed Isabelle to get Sir Dwayne.

It had to be that Isabelle fell off the terrace. Rita walked into the garden to smoke and saw her there. Isabelle looked up and saw Rita's face. Rita moved closer to check on her. Isabelle died. The last thing she saw was imprinted in her memory.

It made sense to me. Maybe there was even proof. Who'd called 911 to report Isabelle's fall? It was probably Rita.

But why show me that moment if it wasn't important?

Maybe it was important to Isabelle. It was her last memory of her life. Maybe that was all that mattered.

If we could've actually talked to Isabelle, asked her questions, we might know the truth now. Why was everything associated with the spirit world so difficult to understand? I didn't like the idea that Isabelle might have as much to say as Wanda, and follow me around the Village, but a simple statement of the killer's identity would've been nice.

I thought that the assault on Rita had something to do with Isabelle's death—but what? Sir Dwayne had an alibi for when Rita was attacked. I didn't know if his time was accounted for during Isabelle's death. The two events felt intertwined in my thoughts.

Chase's cell phone rang at six-thirty the next morning. I'd spent the entire night trying to figure it out and hadn't noticed that gray morning light had crept through the windows.

"Who the hell—?" Chase tried to find his cell phone on the side table and knocked it on the floor.

"It must not be security people." I yawned. "It's not the radio."

It was Detective Almond. He was on his way to the Village to talk to Chase about something new that he'd learned.

"I hope the monks are awake and have coffee ready," Chase said after he'd finished talking. "I don't want to have him in here, and I need a large coffee."

"Why not have him here?" I asked, getting out of bed. "Only we can see the changes the sorcerer did to the apartment. We've had other people from the Village here."

"I don't know. It makes me nervous. I don't want to worry that the apartment is bigger on the inside than it is on the outside." He scrubbed his eyes with his hands. "People in the Village wouldn't care even if they could see it. Detective Almond would."

I hadn't realized that he felt that way. I thought about it while he showered and shaved. He was dressed and ready to go in a few minutes. I watched as he laced his knee-high boots.

"Are you embarrassed about the apartment?" I asked him.

"No." He pushed his braid back on his shoulder as he bent over. "But I also don't dress like this when I go to the police station. I don't like my two worlds colliding. That's all."

I went around and kissed him. "Can I come too?"

"For the coffee or the news?"

"Both. And to spend time with you before the day starts."

"If you can be ready in five minutes."

"Since the Village isn't open yet, I can be ready in two minutes." I threw my pajamas on the floor and put on the denim shorts and tank top I'd been wearing last night. "All I have to do is run a comb though my hair."

"Why are you so awake this morning?" He got to his feet. "Usually, it's all I can do to get you out of bed by eight."

"Don't ask," I yelled from the bathroom as I combed my hair and brushed my teeth.

"You were awake all night thinking about the thing with Isabelle, weren't you?"

"Not just Isabelle—Rita too. I think Madame Lucinda is right about what Isabelle saw." I slipped my feet into sandals.

"What part of that was right?" he asked as we started out of the apartment. "I don't remember anything she said making any sense."

Detective Almond was on the stairs with his hand up to knock on the door. "I see you're ready to go. You're the best, Manhattan. I hope the coffee is good and hot."

He walked past us and into the apartment.

* * *

How did it work? I wondered as I measured coffee into the coffeemaker. I knew it was some kind of spell that the sorcerer had put on the apartment. But the other space was so small—what was Detective Almond seeing as I worked in the much larger kitchen area?

He and Chase were sitting in the living room on two chairs. We didn't even have two chairs in the old apartment. This was the first time I'd stopped to think about it. It was probably because Chase had said something.

"We have some donuts." I smiled at them as the coffee perked. "Would you like a few?"

Detective Almond glared at me. "That whole thing about cops eating donuts isn't true. Besides," he patted his belly, "I'm trying to cut back. My physical is coming up. No cream or sugar for me either, Jessie. Thanks."

I brought my cup, and Detective Almond's, over to the chairs. Chase got his own and filled it with as much milk and sugar as the cup would hold. I sat on the sofa, wondering where it looked like I was sitting through our guest's eyes.

"I'm trying to make a case against Dwayne Barbee, but so far, I keep running into dead ends." Detective Almond slurped his coffee. "Several people saw him come back to the castle before Ms. Martinez was assaulted. They had some kind of tiff after their big make-out session at the hatchet-throwing game that Jessie saw. They both agree on that account. He's off the hook for that."

I was happy about that for Rita's sake, even if she and Sir Dwayne broke up.

"I've looked into the possibility that he could've murdered Ms. Franklin," Detective Almond continued. "He's too big to wear that green shirt we found in the secret passage, but the medical examiner is positive that the material from the shirt matches the material we found in her hand."

"Maybe he didn't do it," I said.

"Whose side are you on anyway?" Detective Almond glared at me. "I discovered something in the course of the investigation that I'm not happy about."

"What's that?" Chase asked with a frown at me.

"We thought Ms. Martinez had phoned for the ambulance after she saw the princess fall. As far as we can tell, she was the first one to see Ms. Franklin on the ground. We've all gone according to that assumption. Then Mr. Barbee tells me during questioning that he called 911 after he went down to the garden. I checked with emergency services, and he was telling the truth. What's up with that?"

Chase glanced at me before he spoke. "Are you sure?"

"You can listen to the tape if you like." Detective Almond slurped more coffee. "It leaves me with a problem. Was Ms. Martinez the first one in the garden or not? If she was, why didn't she call 911? If not, why?"

"Where was Sir Dwayne?" I asked.

"You mean Mr. Barbee?" Detective Almond didn't look happy to realize that I was still there. Maybe I was supposed to get the coffee and disappear. But if this were the old apartment, where would I disappear to?

"Where did he say he was?" Chase facilitated.

"He said he was in her room—one of her chambermaids or whatever you call them—agrees that he was nowhere near the princess when it happened." Detective Almond looked around the kitchen. "You got any plain bagels? I'm really hungry."

"Sorry. We're fresh out," I said. "Are you saying that you think Rita was involved with Isabelle's death now?"

Chapter Twenty

Detective Almond shrugged. "I'm saying this case makes less sense to me now than it did when I started. But that's the way it goes when I have to investigate something here. Is there any place that makes bacon for breakfast around here?"

"We don't do much breakfast in the Village," Chase said. "You know that. What do you want me to do?"

"Ms. Martinez is coming home from the hospital today. Her injuries looked bad but weren't life threatening," Detective Almond told him. "It's possible she knocked herself around to take away any suspicion that she could've been responsible for Ms. Franklin's death. I'd like you to keep an eye on her. I know Rita. She's a nice person—but she's also strong as a horse. She could've thrown Ms. Franklin from the terrace and went down to make sure the job was done."

"That's a terrible thing to say," I told him.

"I've seen people do worse, Jessie." He scanned the

apartment as he got to his feet. "You two are gonna have to do better than this place if you plan to have kids someday. You need something bigger, Manhattan. I'll talk to you later—after I find some bacon."

Chase and I watched him open the door to the apartment and leave.

"Well?" I asked him.

"I guess it looks like the old place to him." He hugged me. "Let's go find some breakfast and some decent coffee."

"Decent? I thought it was pretty good."

"Yeah. Let's go."

We ended up being joined by a large group of Village security guards as we sat at the Monastery Bakery. Several of them were new and had questions about their jobs. The biggest question was when they were supposed to call Chase.

"I expect you to be able to figure out what to do in most situations," Chase told them. "I've decided to choose a supervisor for each shift that the rest of you can call for small things that come up. I know how confusing some of the situations can be. When in doubt, call your supervisor. The supervisors will decide when to call me."

I stared at him with awe and admiration. He'd finally decided to delegate some of his work. I knew it was hard for him. I didn't say anything then, but once we were alone, I threw my arms around him. "You did it! I'm so proud of you. How do you feel?"

"It's not that big a deal." He hugged me and then moved away. "You were right. I've been taking on too much. There are other things I should be focused on."

"You're going to put more time into your patent finding business?"

He frowned. "No. But I told my dad I'd take a look at some stuff for him. He needs an extra set of eyes."

That sounded serious. Chase's father had gone to prison for a short time for fraud. His family had enough money that it hadn't really affected them. I wondered what exactly his father had asked him to do.

"Can I do something to help?" I was hoping he might tell me what was going on.

"No. I can handle it. I'll be working online with Morgan too."

Great. Chase's father and his brother, Morgan, both hated me and didn't want Chase to live at the Village. His mother too, for that matter. I hoped whatever it was would be short term.

I tried not to let it hurt my feelings that he didn't want to tell me everything. I probably wouldn't know what he was talking about anyway. No doubt it was stock market information. I just hoped it was legal stock market stuff. I didn't want Chase to go to jail.

He kissed me. "I'll see you for lunch, Jessie."

I was about to go check on Bill, even though it was early, when I saw Rita coming through the resident's entrance by the Main Gate. She was alone, using a cane to help her walk, her arm in a white sling.

"Let me help you." I took the bag she carried. "How are you?"

"As good as can be expected." She smiled but I could see it was painful. "I had to leave my flowers at the hospital. The taxi driver wouldn't take them."

"I'm sorry. You should have called and we would have picked you up."

"I didn't think about it, Jessie, but thanks for offering."

We walked past the mermaid lagoon. It was empty now—too early for the mermaids. Most residents weren't up yet.

"Detective Almond paid me a call as I was being discharged this morning," Rita said. "I believe he thinks I killed Isabelle. Crazy idea, huh?"

"Crazy. He came to see Chase this morning too."

"Why does he think I killed her?"

"Dwayne is off his hit-list now. I think he knows how you feel about him."

"What do you think, Jessie?"

"I can't imagine you hurting anyone." I didn't hesitate to give my opinion. I wished I could tell her about my vision of Isabelle. I wasn't sure how she'd take it. "There's the thing about you not calling 911, even though you were there right after Isabelle fell. That's what detective Almond is looking at. What happened?"

Rita was uncomfortable. "How does he know? Never mind." She sighed. "I'm sure everyone knows by now."

"What happened?"

"I was standing there, getting ready for a cigarette, looking at the flowers. And she fell. Just dropped down from the terrace. The sound was—I can't describe it. But I knew she was hurt bad, you know?"

I nodded.

"I walked closer when she didn't move, and looked down into her face. I called her name. I think she was already dead."

Not quite. I remembered the last thing Isabelle saw.

"And then I walked away." Rita bit her lip. "God help me. I turned around and went back into the castle. I don't know what I was thinking. It was like I didn't feel anything about her being dead. It wasn't like I thought Dwayne and I could be together if she was dead. I just didn't feel anything."

"What happened then?"

"I walked into the kitchen. Someone rang for a snack, and it hit me what I'd done. I started to call for help, but someone had already called."

"Dwayne."

Rita wiped tears impatiently from her face. "It was stupid and wrong. I know that, Jessie. But I didn't kill her. She was only a kid when she came to work at the castle. I never liked her, but I wouldn't have hurt her."

"Is that what you told the police?"

"Part of it." She smiled. "You know—we keep our secrets here at the Village. The rest that I told you wouldn't have made Detective Almond think any better of me. I'm not sure what to do now."

"I guess just get better and see what happens."

"It's a funny thing," she remarked as we reached the castle gate. "I really felt like the person who attacked me did it because of Isabelle."

"In what way?"

"I don't know." She stopped walking and faced me. Her face was bruised, lips swollen. "I felt like the person was punishing me for what happened, because I left Isabelle there. To begin with, I thought it was Isabelle. It was definitely a woman."

"A woman did this to you?"

"She used a baseball bat or something. She was strong. I didn't get a good look at her, but it was a woman."

Gus was at the gate to the castle. "Ladies."

"Try it, and lose a hand." Rita didn't mince words with him about his habit of pinching butts. "I'm in no mood for your nonsense."

"What's wrong with her?" Gus asked me.

I ignored him, and didn't follow Rita inside. One of the kitchen helpers was there to meet her. She took her bag and helped her into the castle.

Was Rita telling the truth? What she'd done was bad, but not murder. If Sir Dwayne could account for his time when Isabelle was killed and Rita didn't kill her—who did? Was it the same woman who'd attacked Rita?

* * *

Bill surprised me by being up and dressed by the time I'd reached his house. "I'm moving into my own place today," he said. "I feel like I have a new lease on life."

Fred said he felt the same and then fell back on the sofa, snoring.

"I won't miss that guy," Bill said. "I think life in the Village is going to suit me just fine. Let's go get some coffee. Do you have some people lined up to help me move today?"

I didn't have anyone lined up, but I knew I could find a dozen people to take Bill's things from the museum and

Fred's house to his new shop and apartment. "I think it's going to be a great last day of the exhibit. I can't wait for everyone to see your artistry."

Bill threw open the front door and went down like a sack of old laundry on the cobblestones at my feet.

"What's wrong?" I dropped to his side. "Bill? Are you hurt?"

All I could think was that Wanda had done something—hit him in the head, knocked the breath out of him—something to ruin his last day. She was good at that. I hadn't seen her, but that didn't mean she wasn't there.

Bill was curled up on the cobblestones in the fetal position. His eyes, when I locked gazes with him, were desperate. "I can't go out there. What was I thinking? I can't face all those people. There are too many of them. I can't make boots like I used to. I don't know what to do."

"I know what to do." I tried to help him to his feet. "We have to get you down to Madame Lucinda's and get your magic back. You can't keep going this way. The Village has invested in you because of me. We're not going down because you need your elf magic. Come on."

I thought I could get him up, but his legs kept buckling under him. "Stay right here. I'll think of something."

"Maybe she could come here, Jessie." He threw one arm across his face. "I don't think I can go anywhere."

Residents were waking up and going about their morning tasks to get ready for the Main Gate to open. Fairies giggled as they skipped by, and the walking tree we called the Green Man was careful as he practiced on his stilts.

I cut across the King's Highway, running until I'd reached the small stand where visitors could hire a peasant-drawn cart to convey them around the Village. Justin, the peasant who ran the service, was just getting out of bed and pulling on his costume as I ran into his small house. "I need you," I told him. "I need you right now."

It took some bargaining—and the forty dollars I had in my pocket—to get Justin up and moving. I let him pull me to

Fred's house—seemed like a fair trade—and found Bill still on the ground.

"Help me get him in the cart." I got down from the colorful one-person cart.

"That will cost you extra." Justin grinned.

"Have I mentioned that my husband is the Bailiff? Don't make me call him."

Justin dropped the attitude and helped me try to move Bill to the cart. It was difficult since Bill's body had become like a large piece of Jell-O. I grabbed his feet and legs. Justin grabbed his arms and shoulders. But Bill was not only dead weight but floppy dead weight at that.

"Just kill me, Jessie," Bill cried out. "My life is over anyway."

I was about to really lose it when Bart came walking by. "Greetings, my lady. Need you a hand or two?"

"Thank you, sir." I curtsied. "It's either that or we're going to chop him into little pieces and let the dogs have at him."

Bill moaned pitifully but still couldn't move.

Bart grabbed him with one arm and tossed him into the cart. "There you are, lady. Where are you taking him?"

"To get his elf magic back."

"Do you believe it's real after all?" Bart whispered with a smile.

"I don't know," I admitted. "But he can't function without it. We have to go to Madame Lucinda and get it back. I don't want to lose my job because of him."

"Allow me to assist you," Bart offered gallantly.

Justin grinned. "Then you don't need me, right?"

"We still need your cart, and I already paid you to pull it," I reminded him.

Bart stared at Justin and shook one of his large fingers at him. "I can't believe you asked this wonderful lady to pay you for your help, sir. In the Village, we have a code of helping each other. Taking money from a person in need is not part of that code."

"I just thought it would be okay." Justin tried to smile as he glanced at me and then looked contrite when he faced Bart who was at least double his size.

"Not okay at all," Bart said. "Perhaps this will clarify my position."

Bart picked Bill up again, and holding him in his arms like a child, he climbed on the cart and sat down. The sturdy wood creaked and groaned, but it held together. "You may proceed, sir."

Justin stared at me. "You're joking, right? You don't think I can pull both these dudes all the way to the Main Gate, do you? I'm not a pack mule."

Before I could say anything, Bart said, "I'm waiting. Don't keep me waiting too long."

"Okay. Okay." Justin handed me back my forty dollars. "There. All better now."

Bart drummed his fingers on the side of the cart. An audience of residents was watching by then. Justin swallowed hard, took up the brightly painted yoke, and started slowly pulling Bart and Bill down the cobblestones.

Everyone came out to watch the spectacle. They cheered as though it was a parade. I didn't know if Justin could make it all the way to Madame Lucinda's tent, but he managed. He collapsed on the ground, breathing hard when he got there. Bart stepped down from the cart, smiled at him, and then took Bill inside.

I followed them quickly, pushing aside the tent flap. "Madame Lucinda!"

"No need to shout, Lady Jessie. I heard the commotion long before you got here."

Bart gently laid Bill on a black velvet sofa that I could swear had never been there before. It was always amazing watching a man as big as Bart with his butterfly-gentle touch.

"Madame Lucinda." He bowed to her and smiled. "I hope you can help this man. I must go to the castle, but it is always a pleasure seeing you and Buttercup."

Wait! Could he see the dragon too? I never thought to

ask him.

"It is always a pleasure to see you as well, my friend." Madame Lucinda inclined her head elegantly.

Buttercup actually jumped from the shelf where she usually perched to the table. She gazed up at Bart with something approaching a smile on her face too.

"Good morning, Buttercup." Bart scratched under her neck that she held out for him.

"You can see her!" I was very pleased not to be completely crazy.

Bart and Madame Lucinda's heads swiveled toward me. "Of course," he said. "Can't everyone?"

Buttercup growled at me and leapt back to her perch.

"She's not quite used to you, Lady Jessie," Madame Lucinda explained.

I wanted to launch into a diatribe about everything that was weird with Buttercup and her mistress, but it would have to wait. Bart took his leave of us, and Bill rolled on the floor.

"I was afraid something like this would happen. Help me get him back on the sofa, Jessie."

Madame Lucinda and I finally managed to get Bill back on the sofa. He was crying, almost not able to hold up his head. "Maybe I should call an ambulance," I said.

"No need," she told me. "I'll return his elf magic, and he'll be fine."

She brought out a dark blue bottle, waiting to open it until she was standing beside Bill. Once she'd taken off the stopper, a bright light flashed from its deep blue depths. The light illuminated Bill for a moment and then disappeared.

"Was that it?" I asked, a little skeptical. "Was that the elf magic?"

"Indeed it was." She sighed. "Foolish man for thinking he could live without it. If given such a blessing, what man would turn it aside?"

Bill had stopped groaning and slowly sat up. He stared at his hands and feet for a long time. "I'm alive."

"Of course you're alive," Madame Lucinda said with a

touch of irritation. "Lucky for you that I never take magic without saving it. Learn to use it. I shouldn't have to tell you this. Don't ever give it up again."

He hopped to his feet and did a little impromptu jig. "You don't have to worry about me, ma'am. I learned my lesson." He made his ears wiggle and then ran out of the tent.

I felt like falling back on the sofa. There was too much drama and too little sleep. I smiled at Madame Lucinda and bowed my head. "Thank you for your help."

"And how will you use your gift, Jessie?"

"I hope you're not telling me that seeing dead people is my gift. If so, get a bottle and put it inside. I'll be glad to give it up."

She laughed. "You have so much to learn. If you have questions, don't hesitate to come to me."

I thanked her again, yawned, and left the tent. I could tell already that it was going to be a long day.

Chapter Twenty-one

I went back to the Dungeon to shower and get ready for the day. Chase was working. I had the apartment to myself. I had plenty of time, for once. I didn't have to hurry.

I laid out my new violet-colored skirt and blouse. Chase had bought me a darker purple bodice to wear with it. I hummed some music I'd heard from the trio of musicians that had played at the museum opening as I got undressed. Despite everything, life at the Renaissance Faire was great, and I was the luckiest woman in the world to be there with Chase.

I went in the bathroom to shower, and when I came out, my clothes were gone.

I thought maybe I was so tired that I only thought I'd laid out the dress. I looked in the closet—it wasn't there either. Then I thought Chase was back and playing games.

But a quick check of the apartment told me that I was alone. I even thought that Wanda had managed to get back inside. I called her name several times. It was just the kind of stunt she would pull.

But Wanda loved taking credit for the things she did. She didn't answer my summons, and I had to give up on that idea too. What was going on?

I was angry that I couldn't wear my new clothes, and determined to find out what had happened to them. I put my shorts and T-shirt back on and started slowly going through the apartment. Maybe I was so tired that I'd put the dress in another room and then missed it as I walked through.

Nope.

The whole event was really starting to bother me. My clothes didn't magically disappear—although I thought anything was possible. But why my clothes, and my new clothes at that? It didn't make sense.

I walked into the nursery that had been set up by the sorcerer who'd enlarged our apartment. Everyone seemed interested in Chase and I having a baby. The lovely sweet grass cradle that Mary Shift, the Gullah basket weaver had made, was there. There were a few other small things that friends had given us for that day in the future when we might consider having a child.

But no sign of my clothes.

I crossed the carpet to look out the window to the cobblestones below. I felt rather than heard the door to the room close behind me. I looked back, but I was alone.

Again, I saw Isabelle fall from the terrace. I could feel the rush of air on my skin. I fell to the floor with the same impression I'd seen in Isabelle's dying eyes. A long skirt touched my arm, and then I lost consciousness.

* * *

"Jessie! Wake up!" Chase was leaning over me, shaking me and laughing. "I knew you were tired, but you can't sleep now. The museum is open."

My head hurt. I didn't appreciate his humor. Why would he think I'd take a nap on the floor? "Someone was in the apartment. I think it was Isabelle. I saw her fall again, and I think she stole my new purple outfit."

Chase had stopped laughing, but he was still smiling as he helped me up. "You mean the one you have laid out on the bed."

I started to argue with him as we walked into the bedroom. There was my violet skirt and blouse with the dark purple bodice beside it. "What's going on? I think Wanda was in here."

"I don't know. Manny opened the museum and then called to let me know that you didn't show up. Are you okay?"

"No. I'm not okay. I don't want to see Isabelle falling to her death the rest of my life. What does it mean? Why do I keep seeing it happen?"

"I can't believe I'm going to say this—why don't you get dressed and see if you can find Wanda? Maybe she figured out a way in here and you're driving yourself crazy for nothing." He kissed me. "I don't know what we'll do if she can go in and out again."

I made him stay there while I finished dressing. It was almost eleven before we got on the cobblestones. I looked for Wanda, but I didn't see her anywhere. Chase walked to the museum with me.

"I have to work with the jousters," he said. "Will you be all right?"

"I'll be fine." I managed a snarky smile. "If that was Wanda, I want my money back on the apartment remodel from the sorcerer."

Manny was happy to see me. I told him what had happened. He was more upset about it than Chase. "Perhaps you should call law enforcement."

"I told Chase. That's as close to law enforcement as I usually need to go."

"And why didn't he take it seriously?"

"Because he thinks it was Wanda. He could be right. I didn't see anyone, but I know my clothes were missing when I came out of the bathroom. Then they were back when I looked again. Maybe the spell that kept Wanda out of the apartment wore off. It's either that or I'm going crazy. I think I'd rather it be Wanda, but I'm not sure."

He gazed critically at my face. "You do seem rattled. Perhaps some tea from Mrs. Potts would help. Honey is most healing too."

"If you're going, honey cookies would be most healing of all." I smiled. "Thanks, Manny."

He bowed elegantly. Two older women waiting to see Bill took Manny's picture.

"I will never become accustomed to that," he said.

"Then you shouldn't do such cute Ren Faire things."

He scowled as he left for the Honey and Herb Shoppe. I sat down on a chair near the door to give out information about Bill and his new shop to visitors coming into the museum.

Now that Bill had his elf mojo back, he was in great form again. He was flirting and laughing with the ladies as they tried on his boots. He told his stories about his shoemaker ancestors, including his story about Cinderella's glass slippers.

"So my great-great grandfather says to Cinderella's fairy godmother, 'Why glass slippers? They could break and cut her feet.' And the fairy godmother says, 'Because they'll make her big feet look smaller.' Can you believe it?"

The women loved him. They laughed at his jokes and bought his boots like there were no other boots in the world. I didn't know if he really had elf magic or not, but he believed it and thought it made him a better, more interesting person. That was all that mattered.

Manny returned with my tea and honey cookies. He was right too. I felt much better after I'd had them. Maybe my missing clothes were all in my head.

We closed the museum for lunch so all three of us could have a break. Bill was returning to his dart game that I'd interrupted at the pub. Though it still made me shudder to think about it, it was his life. I couldn't keep him out of trouble all the time.

Chase, Manny, and I ate lunch at one of the outdoor picnic tables set in the shade of a huge magnolia tree. I was hoping Wanda might see us there and come by to laugh at what she'd done at the apartment that morning. But she didn't show. I finally gave up and went back to work.

Afternoon crowds at the Village were always morning beach people who came in bikini tops and smelled like sun block. I thought they were probably bored with the ocean and looking for something else to do. I was glad that they'd chosen us instead of shopping on the boardwalk.

Everyone loved Bill and bought so many pairs of sandals that I had to send out for more materials to keep him going.

"This exhibit has done extremely well," Manny said as we surveyed the crowd who watched Bill at his table. "We should have no problem getting a new exhibit."

"I kind of promised Luke Helms at the pipe shop that we'd host him here next. I'll have to run that by Adventureland and see what they think. But I like the idea. It's good to exhibit some of the items made by the older residents too."

"I saw him at the Honey and Herb Shoppe. He seems to be spending a lot of time there. Mrs. Potts was sitting with him. I believe they were holding hands."

"I was right! Maybe that's my gift. Madame Lucinda said I have a gift. I was hoping it wasn't anything to do with dead people."

"Why on earth would you think that?"

I told him about my encounter with Isabelle in the castle garden. "All that, and I don't think I learned anything from her. Detective Almond is investigating Rita now. She admits that she didn't call 911 right away after she found Isabelle in the garden. I don't think she's a killer."

"But how can you be sure? You said both women wanted the red-haired gentleman. Perhaps they fought over him."

"I don't know. Rita could have been the killer and made

it look like someone beat her up, but I've known her for a long time. She's just not that kind of person."

Manny shook his head. "People will do wonderful and terrible things when they are in the throes of passion. You might know Rita when she is herself. You might not recognize her as a woman in love."

I thought about what he'd said the rest of the afternoon. As usual, the day was hot, and we had a quick shower around four p.m. Almost all of the visitors stayed in the Village until the rain had passed. The storm ruined a few of the more outlandish costumes worn by our wannabe actors. If they couldn't stand up to a little rain, they probably wouldn't make it.

The Main Gate closed at six with all the usual fanfare. The visitors leaving that afternoon received a special treat—a visit from King Harold, Queen Olivia, and Princess Pea. They were accompanied by both their retinues, and were in full royal gear. Their ladies and gentlemen gave out a few hundred free passes to the King's Feast on Sunday evening. Most visitors were thrilled to see the royal family and even more excited to receive the free passes.

"Any sign of Wanda yet?" Chase asked as he joined me on the museum stairs overlooking the crowds at the gate.

"Nope. It's been quiet—except for the legions of Bill's fans. He's going to be a hit here, as long as he keeps his elf magic."

He sat beside me. "You think he really has magic?"

"It doesn't matter what I think. He believes, and he's better with it. I think we sold a thousand pairs of sandals to the afternoon beach-bunny crowd."

"That's great. Adventureland is going to know that you can pick great exhibits."

We watched as the crowds slowly dwindled away. Visitors found their transportation home and went their separate ways. Residents began drifting to their homes for the evening. There was a rhythm to life here, as odd as it might be.

Chase's radio went off. There was a small child on top of the rock-climbing wall. No one knew how he got up there, especially not his alarmed parents.

Chase and I exchanged looks—"Wanda!" we both yelled at once.

We raced across the cobblestones to reach the wall. A sizable group of residents and visitors had lingered there to watch the drama.

While Chase began the climb up the wall to get the crying toddler, I searched the crowd. "Wanda?" I whispered her name. "Are you here? Show yourself."

It only took a moment. She appeared to me with a sly smile on her blue face. "Don't tell me you're finally warming up to me, Jessie. After all this time. All I had to do was die to have you like me."

"I knew you'd be here. What's with putting the kid up there?"

She stared at Chase as he climbed the wall. "Don't you love a little drama as the Village is closing? I know I do. The perfect end to a perfect day."

I shook my head. I was never going to change, or understand her. "How did you get back into my apartment?"

"What are you talking about? I haven't been in there since I was banished."

"You were there this morning. You moved my clothes, and made me have that vision of Isabelle again. Don't deny it. How did you do it?"

Her ghastly blue face turned serious. "You should get out of this sun, Jessie. You're obviously overheated. I didn't get into your apartment—even though the entire event you've described sounds like enormous fun. Perhaps your other ghostly friend, Princess Isabelle, is responsible. Two ghosts might be more than you can handle and stay sane. See you later."

She disappeared as a loud Huzzah! went up from the crowd. Chase had reached the child on the wall and was bringing him down safely.

I believed Wanda about her not being in the apartment. I didn't know who else would do such a thing, or why, but I knew her well enough to know she would have rubbed my face in the fact that she'd managed to break through the spell.

Knowing it wasn't her didn't make me feel any better. Wanda was annoying, but at least I understood her. Wondering who else would go to such lengths to scare me was worse. What was going on?

Chapter Twenty-two

The boy was brought safely to the ground. His alternately crying and laughing parents hugged him and kissed him. There were several rounds of Huzzahs! The security guards escorted the remaining visitors to the Main Gate.

As usual, there were a handful of teenagers who'd managed to stay beyond closing time. There were thousands of places to hide in the Village. Some managed not to be seen until morning. Chase never liked when that happened.

He had another meeting with the security guards before dinner. I decided to go to the castle and take another look around the garden and Isabelle's suite. I wasn't sure what I was looking for. It just seemed to me if there were answers to be found, they'd be there.

Gus wasn't at the castle gate again. It wasn't like him to shirk his gatekeeping responsibilities. I didn't plan to mention it to Chase, though, since I knew what was going on. Gus had a right to his own life. Who knew how long this affair of his would last anyway?

I started in the garden. I knew the police and Village security had thoroughly searched this area. There probably wasn't anything left to find. But the scene between Isabelle and Rita haunted me. Manny was right about not knowing a person until you had seen them in love or some other emotional circumstance. I was sure Rita had reacted to Isabelle in a way she would have normally never considered. There was still a chalk outline of Isabelle's stricken form on the stones. The police had made sure everyone knew where it had happened. The reminder would be gone when the maintenance crew cleaned the patio again. For now, it was a terrible tribute.

I looked at the outline and then up at the terrace. Rita and Dwayne were both physically capable of lifting Isabelle and throwing her into the garden. So was Bill for that matter.

Who else was strong enough to do the deed and had a reason to kill Isabelle?

I already knew that Isabelle's retinue was accounted for during that time. It was hard to imagine any of her ladies having the strength to lift her. There were a few jugglers and fools who were always hanging around. Maybe it was one of them.

The garden was close to Gus's post at the castle gate. I heard him return, slightly drunk, if his voice was any indication. Curiosity made me wonder who he was seeing outside the castle. It was unusual not to have heard any gossip regarding his romance. Everyone knew even when the romance stayed behind the castle walls. He'd done a good job hiding it if he was seeing someone who lived in the Village.

I walked through the castle and upstairs to Isabelle's suite. It was dark and empty. I switched on the light. Already changes were being made. There were gallons of pink paint for the walls, and boxes containing Isabelle's personal items. It was a lovely suite of rooms—not surprising that Princess Pea would take them.

No one had touched the closets yet. Isabelle's clothes

were still neatly stored away. Her large bed was still in place too. Those would probably be the next things to go.

I searched through everything that was left—Isabelle's hairbrush, jewelry, and other small intimate items. I opened one of her drawers and found several slutty magazines. Did anyone really know Isabelle? She'd been a pretend princess here for so long. Did she remember who she really was?

I felt something move past me and jumped back a foot or two. My heart was pounding when I saw a dark burgundy gown that had been in the closet just a moment before. It was set out on the bed as though invisible hands had been getting it ready for Isabelle to change clothes.

It reminded me too much of what had happened at the apartment. I felt cold all over and turned to leave.

Dresses, royal ball gowns, riding and street clothes began to move around the room. The material rushed by from the closets to the bed. Some of the garments struck me as I tried to reach the door. The clothes heaped themselves on top of the burgundy gown. They were joined by undergarments, hats, and shoes.

Inside the colorful whirl of clothing, I stifled a scream as I reached the door to the suite.

It wouldn't open. I jerked at it again and again, but it wouldn't budge. I set my back against it, and watched in fascinated horror as the closets emptied themselves on the bed.

"Isabelle! Why are you doing this? What are you trying to tell me?"

There was no reply, and no glowing vision of her. The clothes and accessories kept flying out of the closets and drawers. I didn't understand what she was trying to say. Leave it to her to try to tell me something important with clothes!

"Okay. Clothes. Something about laying out clothes. You want to tell me about your clothes. Is it what you want done with them? Is there something special about your clothes?"

No answer. The clothes that had been in the air on their way to the bed suddenly dropped to the carpet. Maybe I'd correctly guessed some part of the puzzle. I searched frantically through my mind trying to figure out what it was. "I'll help if you tell me what you want."

That was wrong too. The clothes that had been on the bed started coming toward me. I was pelted with satin, lace, velvet, and leather. It only took a few seconds before I was covered in clothing. The shoes kind of hurt as they smacked me.

"All right. That's not what you wanted," I yelled in frustration. "I don't do signs and omens. Please make it plainer for me. You know what you want to say. I don't."

The clothes stopped again. That was a relief. I battled my way out from under them—a six-foot heap of materials that slid down the door when I moved.

The only thing left on the bed was the burgundy gown. It was perfectly laid out with underwear, shoes, and stockings.

I studied it, but I still didn't get it. Did she want me to wear the gown? It wasn't the gown that she was wearing when she'd died.

As I watched, the long gown drifted into the air and moved slowly toward the doors that led to the terrace. It stopped until I could open the door. Then the gown fluttered by me and out onto the terrace.

I followed. The gown reached the railing before it went up and over—stopping only when it had reached the garden. It landed between the white chalk outline where Isabelle had fallen, exactly as her body had.

I stood there looking at it for a few minutes. My imagination wasn't enough to take me where the ghostly gown wanted me to be. If Isabelle wanted me to jump down after it, she was crazier in death than she had been in life.

A terrible feeling of sadness set in. I couldn't tell if it was mine or Isabelle's. I started crying as I looked at the gown in the garden. So many people had claimed to love Isabelle yet none of them had been there for her when she'd been killed. She'd been alone then with only the regrets from her past, and the knowledge that she would never be able to make those things right.

The door to the suite opened, and Victoria, Isabelle's lady-in-waiting entered. I remembered her from Isabelle's visit to the museum, and the castle when she'd talked to Chase about Sir. Dwayne.

She glanced around at the clothes that were thrown everywhere, her expression horrified. "What happened?"

"I don't know" I denied all knowledge as I grabbed the door before it could lock again. "It looked like this when I got here. Sorry."

I got out of there as quickly as I could. I still couldn't believe what had happened. My brain didn't want to take it all in. Between the clothes going wild, and the weird thoughts running through my head about Isabelle's death, I was ready to leave the castle and never go back. I needed time to think about what I'd seen.

Trying to avoid facing Gus, I sneaked out one of the side doors. I knew that it led to the supply area and into a parking lot for deliveries. I took a deep breath when I had reached the narrow passage between Stylish Frocks and Mirror Lake. The area was closed to the public, but residents sometimes went out of the Village this way when the Main Gate was backed up with visitors. The delivery area also led to the parking lot where residents kept their vehicles.

I ran full tilt into Sir Dwayne. We were the only ones in the parking lot. His hands went out to steady me before I could lose my balance.

"Lady Jessie. I was hoping to see you. Perhaps this is a bad time?"

Chapter Twenty-three

Out of the frying pan?

I couldn't think of a worse time! I just wanted to go home.

"I'm sorry, Sir Dwayne." Twilight was beginning to fall on the large, empty parking lot. It wasn't a good place to confront a man who had only recently had been intent on kidnapping me. "Chase just called. I was in the castle. I'm sure he's looking for me right now."

Even to my frightened ears, it sounded lame. I couldn't think of what else to say to him. I wanted him to know I wasn't out here alone—well, technically I was—but there were people who cared about me. I wasn't alone.

"Isn't that one of Isabelle's gowns?" he asked.

I looked down. I was wearing the burgundy gown that I'd seen drop into the garden from the terrace. How was that even possible? I couldn't wear Isabelle's clothes. It was insane, and yet, I was wearing it.

I wanted to scream and demand to know what was

happening, but I had to stay calm—at least while I was facing Sir Dwayne. Maybe he wasn't Isabelle's killer. Maybe he was.

"Yes." I managed to sound cool despite my fear. "They're getting rid of her clothes. I decided to take this one, you know, to remember her by. I've always admired it."

"I can't believe you'd want something to remember Isabelle. As I recall, the two of you were never even friendly toward each other."

"All the more reason to mourn her, sir." I buried my face in the sleeve that smelled strongly of Isabelle's perfume. "We never truly had a chance to know each other."

I tried to scoot by him, but he put out his good hand to stop me. The other arm was in a sling like Rita's.

"You seemed hurried, lady," he observed.

"I am late for an important event."

"And you seem afraid."

Just let me go, you big ape!

"Should I be afraid, Sir Dwayne?"

"Not of me, lady." He bowed gallantly, and swept his good arm toward me. "I mean you no harm."

"Then allow me to pass, sir. I am weary and must be on my way."

"Lady Jessie, please allow me to express my apologies for what happened between us. I was desperate, and desperate men do foolish things. I'm leaving the Village, and I wanted to tell you how sorry I am that the unfortunate event happened between us. I have always admired you."

Trying not to be thrown by his sweet words, I moved out of his reach. "I completely understand. I hope your future is bright. Good evening, sir."

"My future is brighter since you and the Bailiff decided not to press charges against me. The police have released me, even though Adventureland fired me. I didn't expect to get away with my regrettable actions completely." He smiled and held out his hand to me. "Thank you. I hope you'll convey my sentiments to the Bailiff."

I hadn't given it another thought. Chase must have taken me at my word that I wouldn't press charges and then told Detective Almond that he wouldn't either. I was surprised and pleased.

And I just wanted to get out of the parking lot and back to the Dungeon.

"Think nothing of it. I've been in desperate circumstances myself. I sincerely hope everything works out for you. I'm sorry you have to leave the Village."

"Thank you for that. I've learned my lesson, I hope. No more princesses for me."

I tried to laugh at that, more at ease with Dwayne after talking to him. But I still felt threatened. Maybe he didn't mean me any harm, but there was something there that kept me ill at ease. I had the same feeling I normally had when I was watching a scary movie. I knew the killer was there. I felt someone sneaking up even though I couldn't see anyone.

Dwayne didn't seem to notice anything. He began talking about his life and his plans for the future. "First of all, I appreciate that you don't think I killed Isabelle. The police aren't as sure. I can't leave Myrtle Beach, even though I lost my job, until the case is settled. I'm from Ohio, you know. Columbus. My folks still live there. I was thinking I might go home for a while. Recuperate, you know?"

"That sounds like a wonderful plan, sir. I wish you much good fortune."

"I was looking for a bottle of wine for Isabelle that day. The shoemaker was there in her suite. I knew she'd led him on and was about to cut him off. She'd gotten what she wanted. She didn't need him anymore."

I told myself not to engage him any further, but I couldn't help myself. "Weren't you worried about how he'd take it?"

"No. Isabelle had a way of making her wishes known without hurting you. I knew I was on the way out too. We'd had some fun. She was in the market for someone new. I was relieved in some ways. She was high maintenance and a lot of drama."

"And when you came back from getting the wine?"

"She'd already fallen into the garden." He shook his head. "The shoemaker was gone. Only one of her ladies was still in her suite." He stared at the burgundy gown I was wearing. "You know, I think she was laying out that gown for Isabelle to wear for dinner that night."

"Which lady was it?"

"I'm not sure, Lady Jessie. They all look the same to me."

I thanked him for the information and urged my feet to move.

He put his good arm around me and planted a quick kiss on my lips. "Just to say goodbye."

"Goodbye, Sir Dwayne. Good fortune." I walked around him, finally, and got away.

It had to be the lady-in-waiting, Victoria! It must have been her green shirt that Isabelle ripped, the one we'd found in the passageway. Victoria had been so quick to give Sir Dwayne an alibi. It was right there all the time—there was someone besides Rita who was in love with Isabelle's lover.

I heard a muffled voice as I was passing the Dutchman's Stage. I don't know why it alerted me. There was plenty of music, laughter, and conversation around me from people sitting outside the pubs and houses.

This was none of those things. It was more a whisper, a sigh. I glanced toward the stage. It was empty. No one was rehearsing or hanging out there. I didn't see anything unusual or hear the odd sound again.

I kept walking toward the Dungeon.

My thoughts were still on the ghostly clothing at the castle. Maybe Isabelle was trying to tell me that it was one of her ladies who had killed her. Specifically, the woman who'd laid out the burgundy gown for her to wear to dinner. The same burgundy gown I was mysteriously wearing after my trip to her rooms. Was Isabelle using the reference to clothes to try to tell me what had happened?

I quickened my pace on the cobblestones, hoping Chase was home so I could tell him everything that had happened.

If Victoria hadn't already left the Village it would be a good idea to gather everyone at the castle right away. She might leave before Chase could talk to her. I couldn't prove anything from my feelings or my ghostly clothing experience. Someone else would have to make her admit what she'd done, or find valid proof that she'd done it.

I wished I had my cell phone. It would make me feel better, safer, to talk to Chase while I was trying to get home. I'd left it at the Dungeon today of all days.

One minute I was thinking about Chase, and the next I was on the ground. Something hard had come out of nowhere and hit me on the side of the head. The blow knocked me down and scrambled my thoughts, but I didn't lose consciousness.

"You had to try to take him, didn't you?" a whispered female voice demanded. "You have a man. You should've stuck to him."

I was being dragged off the main walkway and behind the Dutchman's Stage. The trees were thick and damp in the twilight as we were hidden from lights that were coming on around the Village.

"What are you talking about?" My words were slurred. I could barely make sense of my thoughts. "Victoria?"

"I'm the woman who belongs with Dwayne. Not you. Not Rita. And certainly not Isabelle. None of you love him as I do. When we leave the Village, I'll be with him. You'll be a rotting pile of flesh for them to find back here."

"Look, I don't blame you for killing Isabelle. She was a terrible person. I couldn't stand her either." I hoped to draw her attention away from killing me. "How did you manage it? I know she was small, but you must be very strong."

There was another swing of whatever weapon she was holding. I could barely make out that it was large and wooden. It wasn't a baseball bat. What is it?

I yelled in pain as the weapon hit my arm. I was sure it

was broken. She sat on top of me like some demon, her hands over my mouth and nose.

"Shut up. Just die, will you? I need to leave with Dwayne."

She put the weapon down and put all her effort into covering my nose and mouth with her hands. I beat at her with my one good arm and kicked my feet, but I couldn't throw her off. The burgundy gown hampered my efforts.

Why did I put it on?

I could hear the sounds of my heart beating fast. My breath stuck in my burning lungs.

Wanda—or at least her head—appeared over the top of the woman's left shoulder. "What trouble you can find, Jessie. I was just out looking for something fun to do, and here you are. Who is this person anyway? I can see she wants to kill you. I know the feeling. I'm not sure I'm happy about you being dead now. We've become quite friendly, haven't we? Even though it happened after my unfortunate demise."

I blinked my eyes and tried to encourage her to do something to get the killer off me. There wasn't much time. I was fading away.

Maybe this is death.

I was surprisingly calm about it. I didn't have the energy left to kick my feet or try to get free. I lay there, staring up at the leaves. My mind was drifting. I'd stopped fighting for breath.

"Oh for goodness sake," Wanda said. "You can't just lie there and die, Jessie. Do something. You've always been good at last minute saves. Think how terrible it will be for poor Chase to find you back here. You've let the fight go out of you. Do something now."

But there was nothing I could do. Part of me still wanted to live. Part of me was letting go. I couldn't feel the pain in my arm anymore. This is it.

"Stay here, love," Wanda instructed. "I think I have an idea."

Why don't you just knock her off me? You move things

all the time. Stop her from killing me.

But Wanda always has her own games to play. Just saving me from a killer wasn't enough fun.

I heard the whinny of a horse close by. It sounded startled. A voice followed that yelled out and then tried to sooth the animal.

"The cavalry has arrived!" Wanda announced before she disappeared again.

I was sure I'd taken my last breath when I heard Katharina's voice. "What's going on here? Hey! Let her go!"

I felt the skirmish as the new knight knocked my assailant off me. I rolled over in the damp grass, coughing and sputtering. My arm hurt so bad that I wanted to cry, but I couldn't take the chance that my attacker might manage to get past Katharina.

I forced myself to my feet and dizzily searched for the weapon that had been used to knock me down. I felt it on the grass and picked it up in my good hand.

Katharina was without a sword or lance. She wasn't wearing armor. Her only weapons were her fists and legs. She was strong and much larger than Victoria, but I still had the impression that it was a battle for her to try to vanquish our common foe.

I staggered toward where the two women were fighting and hit the smaller woman with the wooden cudgel. She dropped to her knees. Katharina threw a net over the top of her. For good measure, I hit the woman on her knees again.

"Double tap," I said to her. "Always a good idea with zombies and crazy women."

"Jessie!"

I heard Katharina call my name—and then nothing. The fog I'd tried to keep away encompassed me. It was over.

Chapter Twenty-four

I was in the castle again—in Isabelle's suite—lying on her bed.

No one else was there.

I remembered my broken arm. But it didn't hurt anymore—didn't seem to be broken after all. I moved it experimentally as I got off Isabelle's bed and walked around the room.

Why am I here?

There was a light on the terrace. I opened the glass door and walked out. Isabelle was standing in the light, or the light was coming from her. I wasn't sure which. The one thing I was sure of was that she was dead. I might have been wrong about my arm being broken, but I was sure about that.

She turned to face me, dressed in the same outfit she'd been wearing when she died. She even had Bill's magic slippers on her feet. "Jessie. Thank you for everything you've done. I wouldn't have thought you'd care one way or another about what happened to me. I guess I trusted the wrong people. Maybe you and I could've been friends—if you hadn't stolen Chase from me."

"Isabelle, even dead you're wrong. I didn't steal Chase. You lost him, and he and I found each other. You have only yourself to blame. I thank you for that." I nodded respectfully. I was dealing with a ghost after all.

"Perhaps." She smiled radiantly. "Anyway, I just wanted you to know. I'm glad you aren't dead too. You might not believe it, but I cared deeply for Chase. I'm glad he still has you."

"Thank you, Isabelle. I'm sorry about what happened to you."

"Me too. On the other hand, I don't need magic slippers to fly. Goodbye Jessie."

I watched as she slowly drifted off the edge of the terrace, into the trees and the night, before she disappeared. I know I should've been in awe at seeing her, but all I could think about was that she wouldn't be hanging around the Village like Wanda.

I was going to have to work on my attitude. I couldn't let one wicked ghost ruin my whole life.

And then I was awake. Really awake. The pain in my broken arm was excruciating. My head hurt so bad that I thought it might pop off, and my lungs were still burning from the abuse Victoria had given them. I could barely breathe despite the oxygen mask on my face. I was lying on the cobblestones, but it was only a moment before two paramedics lifted me and put me on a stretcher.

"I'm her husband." Chase's voice was tortured. "I want to go with her."

"Sure," one of the paramedics said.

"Wait!" I glanced around the crowd of residents that surrounded me and moved the oxygen mask. "Where's Katharina?"

"I'm right here, Jessie." She took my good hand and smiled into my face. "You're going to be fine."

"What about you?" I asked. "Are you okay?"

"She was a mean little witch, but I'm not damaged. Between us, we took her down. Thank goodness Firefox was spooked by something just as I was about to ride by the Dutchman's Stage. I've never seen him act that way before. I actually lost control of him. He ran right to where you were and then threw me off. I've never been thrown from a horse before. It was like he knew what was going on."

I heard Wanda's laughter, but she didn't appear. I wasn't sure why she'd bothered saving me, but I was grateful. If there was a price to pay for it in the future, I'd be willing to pay it.

Chase leaned close to me as he replaced the oxygen mask. "We have to go to the hospital. Your arm is broken, and you might have some other injuries."

"Wait a minute!" I removed the mask again as the paramedics started moving toward the Main Gate. "I have to know what she was using. It wasn't a baseball bat."

Rita was there. She brought the weapon—complete with both our blood on it. "You'll probably recognize this now that she isn't trying to kill you with it. They used them in the laundry when they had the old washtubs. You remember?"

I touched the wood cudgel. "I remember. They were stored in the basement. Who knew they could do so much damage?"

Detective Almond snatched it from both of us. "That's evidence in two assaults, if you don't mind. I have a confession from Isabelle's maid. It seems Sir Dwayne was the cause of all this. Not sure he even knew it." He glared at the paramedics. "Get her out of here. I think she's caused enough trouble for one night."

* * *

I was back at the Village in a few days. Manny had stepped in splendidly to make sure Bill's personal items and shoemaking supplies were moved from Fred's house and the museum. Bill's new shop and housing looked wonderful. Bewitching Boots was going to be a hit.

The king and queen threw a party at the castle to celebrate Bill's new shop and to welcome the group of new performers to the Village. Out of three hundred actors who'd auditioned, fifteen were chosen to become full-time residents. Another twenty were tagged to be part-time actors with a chance of being full-time in the future.

The throne room was full of older residents rubbing elbows with newer ones. A huge feast had been laid out by the kitchen staff. Rita directed her workers, despite her injuries from Victoria.

I could see there were several interesting new characters that would be roaming the cobblestones. Some of the actors were a little chagrined to be taken on to replace others who'd left instead of being able to create new characters, but everyone seemed happy to be there. The big, white angel had made the cut as a new character with his questionable 'costume.' So had some steampunk characters.

Chase came to me with a glass of champagne for my good hand. "I have secured a small table for us to share, my lady. Please accompany me."

His words matched his blue velvet doublet and black satin breeches. He even wore the jaunty new blue velvet cap I'd bought him for his birthday. It was a good fit.

He'd helped me into my blue velvet gown that made sure everyone knew we were a couple. He'd been wonderful with everything since I'd been injured, even though he'd spent a lot of time on the phone and the internet with his brother and father. Chase still wouldn't talk about what they were doing. I tried not to worry.

We'd given our statements to the police—no way I wasn't pressing charges against Victoria. I didn't know what would come of that, but I hoped she would be put somewhere she couldn't hurt anyone again.

One thing I hadn't mentioned to anyone—not even Chase. I'd found Isabelle's purple velvet cloak in my closet when I got home from the hospital. It was the same one I'd admired in her closet after she'd died. I didn't ask how it got there. I accepted it as a token from her. Maybe that was crazy, but it had been a crazy time.

Chase and I sat at the table he'd managed to find in the crowded hall. He went to fill our plates at the banquet table, and Bill joined me.

"I'm glad you're up and around, Jessie. Business is so good. I can't thank you enough for bringing me here. And look—the Village costume shop ordered sandals for all the fairies. I think you'll like them. I have a pair for you too."

As I watched, several fairies that were flirting and carrying on did a few pirouettes. One of them laughed as she leaped at least five feet straight into the air, whirling madly as though she really had wings.

Bill smiled and winked at me. "Elf magic. It works every time."

About the Authors

Joyce and Jim Lavene write bestselling mystery together. They have written and published more than 60 novels for Harlequin, Berkley and Gallery Books along with hundreds of non-fiction articles for national and regional publications.

Pseudonyms include J.J. Cook, Ellie Grant, Joye Ames and Elyssa Henry

They live in rural North Carolina with their family, their cat, Quincy, and their rescue dog, Rudi. They enjoy photography, watercolor, gardening, long drives, and going to our local Renaissance Fair.

Visit them at:

www.renaissancefairemysteries.com
www.joyceandjimlavene.com
www.Facebook.com/JoyceandJimLavene
Twitter: https://twitter.com/AuthorJLavene
Amazon Author Central Page:
http://amazon.com/author/jlavene

CPSIA information can be obtained at www.ICGtesting.com
Printed in the USA
LVOW10s2320040914

402557LV00016B/203/P